D1482302

WITHDRAWN

DAN YACK

DAN YACK

BLAISE CENDRARS

Translated from the French by
Nina Rootes

Michael Kesend Publishing, Ltd.
New York

Translated from the French Dan Yack (Le plan de l'aiguille)

First American publication 1987
© Editions Denoël, Paris 1927
Published in Great Britain by Peter Owen Ltd 1987
English translation © Peter Owen Ltd 1987

Library of Congress Cataloging-in-Publication Data

Cendrars, Blaise, 1887-1961.
Dan Yack.

I. Title.
PQ2605.E55D3613   1987   843'.912   87-25971
ISBN 0-935576-22-3

ISBN 0-935576-22-3

Manufactured in the United States of America

TRANSLATOR'S NOTE

When I was studying Cendrars's novel, *Le plan de l'aiguille*, with an English translation in mind, it occurred to me that it was cruel to the hero, and frustrating for the reader, to leave Dan Yack high and dry, as Blaise himself leaves him at the end of the novel. Fortunately, the publishers were able to arrange that we should add, in the form of an Epilogue, an extract from *Les confessions de Dan Yack*, which rounds off the whole Antarctic phase of Dan Yack's history. This is written in the first person singular, but otherwise seems to belong happily where we have placed it. I hope that I may be forgiven for lifting it out of its original context.

Nina Rootes

TO ABEL GANCE

It is to you, my dear Abel, that I dedicate this novel, which is not a work of the intelligence, or even of the sensibilities, but one of brute instinct and animality.

Do not look for a new art formula in these pages, or for a new style of writing, but rather for the expression of tomorrow's general state of health: *man will discard reason.*

'He who would be an angel, becomes a beast.'
Long live man!

Peïra Cava, December 1919   BLAISE CENDRARS

Postscript. All the philosophies are not worth one good night of love, as I believe Shakespeare said.

                                                                B.C.

PART ONE

HEDWIGA

A gramophone blared out a popular tune.

Revolving discs of coloured light, set in motion by ventilators on the ceiling, absorbed the dancing couples and projected their images in dizzy, reeling silhouettes. Voices from every country, the national anthems of every nation on earth, rang out. The arc lamps threw back dazzling reflections from the mirrors and the women spun like humming-tops.

Champagne corks popped in all directions.

The burnished copper horns of the music-machine reared up like four monstrous, greedy mouths, dominating the sea of waving flags and the livid blinking of the electric illuminations.

There was a great burst of laughter as Dan Yack fell and skidded right across the polished parquet on his shoulder-blades. A mad scamper as people rushed to pick him up, and then the liveried footmen escorted him out, closing the flashing doors of the ballroom behind him.

Dan Yack screwed in his monocle and, clasping the handrail of the banisters with both hands, descended the grand staircase of the club, coming down hard on his heels at each step.

The gilt rods that held the red carpet in place stabbed his brain, as painful as darts, and each tread crumbled beneath his feet like a rotting springboard. He felt as if he were performing a dangerous high-wire act, suspended in mid-air above the watching, earth-bound faces and caught in the spotlight that criss-crossed before sinking away into the distance. He was hot. He reached the foot of the staircase in a kind of cloud, his eyes filled with multicoloured confetti, his chest thumping to the rhythmic racket of the fête, his whole body drenched in sweat.

He was trembling.

Porters crowded round him. Their uniforms were adorned with black frogging and each man had a peacock's feather stuck in his

astrakhan cap. One handed him his cane, another his hat, a third his
gloves. Exaggeratedly, like an idiot, he thanked them, nodding his
head in appreciation and gently applauding them with the tips of his
fingers. They smiled, winked in amusement, poked him amiably in the
ribs and pushed him towards the exit. With glazed eyes, fuddled
gestures and legs as flossy as silk, Dan Yack put up a show of
resistance. Leaning back into the arms that supported him, he sang in
a little, nasal voice:

> ... *et benedictus fructus ventris tui* ...
> *A-a-a-men.*

Suddenly he broke free and catapulted himself towards the door.
Amongst the ornamental plants an areca palm stood up like a heron
on one leg. Dan Yack slashed it off with his cane and went out,
bareheaded, bearing the palm in his hand. As he passed the
dumbfounded commissionaire, he thrust it into his face and the man
dropped his baton. The handle hit the ground with a sound like a pea-
shooter going off. A startled carriage-horse set off at a gallop and,
when the flunkeys laughed, the sound of their laughter ripped the
pure veil of the morning; it was like a violation.

Now Dan Yack was in a lamentable state, sitting in the middle of the
street in the shadow of the high black buildings of the Arsenal. He was
bathing in horse-piss and rolling balls of smoking dung between the
palms of his hands.
  The Neva flowed past at eye-level.
  The rushing current swept the timber-barges down at full speed;
crouched and menacing, they ploughed through the close-packed
waves that were ruffled up the wrong way by the harsh wind of dawn.
Sudden shivers rippled the wet fur of the river as it stretched itself
nervously and arched its back. Norwegian steamers miaowed at the
tops of their voices. The rack-toothed jaws of the swing-bridges
opened silently and the small packet-boats fled in disarray, bouncing,
like dolphins terrorized by the approach of a squall.
  All at once the sky billowed like a sail.
  And suddenly the world keeled over, listed, loomed larger and
nearer, began to run before the wind, then tacked, turned in its own
length, shuddered and scudded away again with the wind, into the

distance, shipping heavy seas. In the squall, everything turned black, foundered, dissolved. Fat buoys bobbed past, while the city floated in the spray.

Five minutes later, the river was like a great body covered in goose-pimples, hanging head downwards, legs splayed in the air, thighs gaping as if someone were holding them apart. Obligingly, an island leaned over it and shook itself amidst its long trails of mist. The river was seized with labour pains, glittering forceps induced the water, which was streaked with blood; at last, the sun was delivered, fine, bonny and red-faced. The clouds rushed at it, caught hold of it, plunged it into a tub of starch, and, when it emerged from their embrace, it was suddenly higher up the sky and looked as if it had been bleached.

Dan Yack started.

He felt he had witnessed a prodigious spectacle. He was bowled over by it. Aiming his palm, he took a pot-shot at the clouds and shot them down.

Once more, the entire aspect of things changed, fixing itself for ever in his memory. He saw everything in a raw, crude light. The deserted quay. The humble linen drying on the deck of the imperial yacht. Three sailors singing in a boat.

Dan Yack burst out laughing and yelled insults at them.

Then he set off again at a run.

. . . *et benedictus fructus ventris tui* . . . he sang to the tune of a song he remembered hearing on the gramophone.

He beat time frenetically with his palm.

The fiacres were coming back after a night on the Islands. From the direction of the Stock Exchange he could hear 50,000 clogs drumming, louder and ever louder, as they crossed the pontoon-bridge; naval pennants were clacking in the wind like castanets. An occasional motor car hove into sight. Leaping and bounding, Dan Yack moved on through all this racket. He enjoyed the sensation of dancing to the selfsame rhythm that was rousing and awakening the city. To his eyes everything appeared joyful: colours, lights, life; the drunks slumped in the backs of the fiacres, the enormous tart escorted by two slender officers of the guard, the decorated carriage, the grinning limousine.

. . . *A-a-a-men!* he intoned, crossing the flow of vehicles that threatened to sweep him on towards the Nevsky Prospect, where the first tram was jingling in the morning air.

Coming out behind the Winter Palace, Dan Yack suddenly fell silent. He felt uneasy again. His legs sagged. He was overwhelmed by fatigue. An infinite sadness took hold of him, drained him, blew him up again, oppressed him. He staggered as far as the Bridge of Sighs. He dumped himself down right in the middle of the hog's back, careless of the carriages that brushed past him. A *gardavoï* rushed up to him, then, recognizing this famous reveller who was the envy of all St Petersburg, discreetly withdrew.

Dan Yack experienced the sensation of rising up into the air like an observation balloon. A cable held him back, painfully, like something anchored in the marrow of his bones. A weight. A steam-winch creaked. His nerves were stretched to breaking-point. His heels left the ground, fell back, then rose up again, very gently.

Little by little, this movement became more pronounced. It affected his calf muscles, his shins, his knees and, finally, his thighs.

Now Dan Yack was marking time on the spot and flapping his arms. Even his head was wagging. It seemed to inflate and float away on its own.

Once more, he burst out laughing.

And all the sounds of the city fell on him again. Amplified, dream-like, they reached full pitch. They poured out of every street, charged round every corner at breakneck speed. Carriages flew past like a sudden draught of wind, cars hurtled by, motors roared, wheels spun. High over the rooftops the wind was a turbine engine.

But above all this he could hear the resounding thud of a steam-hammer. His heart. His anxiety. All of a sudden Dan Yack knew why he was there, what he was waiting for and what was waiting for him. Clip, clop! Clip, clop! He recognized the long strides of his mare, Iskra. And he swung round abruptly.

At that precise instant a vehicle bore down on him. A rubber-tyred wheel crushed the tip of his patent-leather pumps. Saliva from the horse's mouth flicked into his eye. The coupé was already dropping down from the hump of the bridge. A minuscule, heavily ringed hand had let fall a gold cigarette-holder. By the time Dan Yack had picked it up, the carriage had already disappeared.

'What a splendid animal that Iskra is!' he said to himself, shaking the delicate, jewel-encrusted trinket he had just picked up.

And while he was extracting a slip of paper from the amber mouthpiece, his mind dwelt on this mare, which no longer belonged to him. Twenty-five thousand roubles. He recalled the shrewd eye of the previous owner. The installing of the mahogany horse-box. The groom, Samuel O'Dorne. Long live Scotland! The sulky. The sheaf of orchids and the jockey's colours, green and silver. The Grand Prix for trotters. Hedwiga's passion. The handsome walking-cane she had given him.

'Damn! I've left it at the club, I must telephone,' Dan Yack said to himself as he reread the crumpled note for the third time.

A moment later, still reading, he thought: What a bitch Hedwiga is! She didn't even show her face to say goodbye to me. She might at least have leaned out a little way. . . .

And, rereading Hedwiga's note for the hundredth time, he thought of nothing now but his racehorse, his beautiful mare, Iskra, which he would never see again. For he must leave. He was sure of that now. He remembered making this decision. Everything had been prepared for the two of them to go away together. He must leave this very day. He would not alter his plans in the slightest. But he would go alone. *Tant pis.* He also remembered having sent a cable, announcing his imminent arrival, in reply to the telegram from the notary informing him of the death of his old uncle, Carlos, of the firm of William and William, Shipowners, of Liverpool.

My dear Danny,
My beloved,

The Prince knows all about us. I have told him everything. Today he is taking me to his estates in the country. We are to be married in three months' time. I have thought it over very carefully. I am sure the child I am carrying in my womb is his. Never forget that I have loved you very dearly. For your sake I committed a thousand follies. But - and this is the opinion of all your friends, of everyone who knows you - you are a little too crazy. I forgive you for everything. Really, though, I couldn't have left with you today. I had no right. I had no right to make the Prince suffer, he is a good man and has been waiting for me for such a long time, making no demands. And one can at least rely on him. I hear you have lost at cards again - a fortune! Trust me, and listen to the advice of a friend who still loves you tenderly, who has always defended you and will continue to do so against, and in the face of, everyone - don't gamble any more, you will end up ruining yourself. It is high time you took things seriously. Like the Prince, who is very serious. He even says what a good fellow you are. Ah, as if I didn't know it - only too well, alas! I beg you, don't look at me like a spoilt child, with those big sorrowful eyes of yours, and don't tell me you are inconsolable on my account. I wouldn't be able to resist the desire to come and kiss you. I count on you never to seek me out or try to see me again.

Hedwiga

PS. The love we once shared I now give to your mare. You know, that was really chic, making me a present of Iskra. I'm taking her with me today. The Prince says it will not be in the least inconvenient. No one but you would do such madcap things. Oh, my dearest!

Your dwidwi

EDINBURGH. M.O. 2889. 2 SEP. 04. 11 A.M. DAN YACK WILLIAM ESQ., BRITISH EMBASSY, ST PETERSBURG. IT IS WITH DEEP REGRET THAT WE ANNOUNCE THE DEATH OF YOUR UNCLE CARLOS YACK WILLIAM OF THE FIRM OF WILLIAM AND WILLIAM SHIPOWNERS STOP FUNERAL FRIDAY STOP YOUR PRESENCE INDISPENSABLE YOU ARE SOLE HEIR

STRAITH ATTORNEY

'Good morning. What are you doing here?'
'May I come in and use the phone?'
'Of course, come in, please. Mind the step.'
The door of The Stray Dog opened. Pronine stepped back to let Dan Yack in. By now there were not many people left in the cabaret. Furs piled on a table, a fleet of galoshes. Women sitting in armchairs. A few men, every one of them sprawled on the floor. The smoke in the place made one astigmatic. It distorted one's vision. The artistes on the stage moved in the distance, then suddenly loomed nearer, appearing deformed, as if in an aquarium. Strange tropical fish swam up from the depths and climbed along the walls, becoming iridescent beneath the slope of the glass ceiling. These were the luminous pictures by Jakovlev, Ssoudaïkine and Grigoriev. The heat melted everything as if it were greasepaint and, at the bottom of each glass, a tiny electric light bulb floated on a lifebelt of lemon-rind. Like the Indian pearl-divers of Lake Titicaca, people were breathing with the aid of two straws. They were all squatting in an ocean-bed slime of crimson plush and polar bear-skin. Little globules of ether and soda burst against their

cheekbones. Eyes winked. All the faces were crusty, cracked, and sizzling like a drop of opium on the end of a needle. Some of the women were like whipped cream and their mouths, when one could see them, were purplish, like candied fruits; others were as frothy as champagne, or fluffy, like brushed wool. Their laughter was nauseating and, as it rose above one's knees, one fought against it like seasickness. Pitching and nausea. The beautiful Oletschka and that unspeakable little Kiki capsized in a fit of the giggles. Trays circulated, bearing more and more glasses and undulating bottles. The waiters, who moved like silent algae, were dressed in tight-fitting breeches of heavily corded green silk. Each wore a wig of Veronese green. Pronine alone wore one of parrot blue. Just at this moment it was Teffi who was on stage. Every part of her not covered by her black gown, with its long train - her breasts, the ganglions of her neck, her head that one longed to slap, with its dirty, roguish little face all puckered up, her blackened eyes - resembled a bunch of garlic. She was singing the popular song of the moment: 'Polire! Lustrare!'[1]

> Quando fummo sulle scale, piccol' moll',
> La mi prese il cazzo in mano, piccol' moll',
> La mi disse, Capitano,
> Sali! Sali!
> Sali, sali, sali, sali, sali, sul sofà piccol' moll'.[2]

Her appeal was all in that raw voice of hers that gave off the sacrosanct odour of Naples.

'Polire! Lustrare!'

Dan Yack simply crossed the room, holding his nose, as if he were crossing a fish-market exposed to the midday sun, a market-place full of detritus, ordure, swarms of flies, cheese rinds, gutted fish, putrefying melons and puddles of chlorine. He took refuge in the telephone booth, but not before, in his haste, he had skidded on some disgusting fruit-peel and almost stretched his length on something even more revolting: a carcase of nocturnal vice, bloated like carrion,

1 'Polire! Lustrare' = literally 'Polish! Burnish'. - N.R.
2 When we were on the stairs, little tart,
   You took my prick in your hand, little tart,
   You said to me, Captain,
   Climb up! Climb up!
   Climb, climb, climb, climb, climb up on the sofa, little tart!

its four hoofs thrashing, was making the beast with two backs in the full glare of three spotlights. Dan Yack's precipitous retreat had unleashed a wild laugh; glasses and bottles shattered into smithereens. Through the padded door of the telephone booth he could hear the room deliriously yelling his name to the tune of 'Anglitschane maladiétze' . . .

He was all the more furious because Hedwiga, whose number he was ringing, did not reply.

He became impatient, nervous. He cried, he wept, he implored. In vain. Nothing answered him except, at the other end of the line, a busy, deafening ringing that drowned in its own noise.

He fell to his knees.

He clutched hold of the receiver.

'Hedwiga! Hedwiga!'

He was very unhappy. Everything around him was spinning. His drunkenness swamped him again. He lost all sense of reality. Everything was turning round. He felt nothing but his own misery.

His eyes roved over the walls of the booth, painted with obscene water-colours by Elena Petrovna. A woman spread-eagled beneath four banana trees, each limb firmly tied to one of them, while an enraged elephant violated her with his trunk. A group of naked gentlemen, each wearing a monocle and with the same tattoo beneath the right breast, making a chain, a *daisy chain* on the pearly beach of an atoll. An adolescent gratifying himself beneath the sucker of a starfish in a landscape of madrepores. Three young girls rising out of the sea in an early morning scene. A long blind snake penetrated, united, tied together and interlaced their bodies and re-emerged from all their natural orifices, making them writhe as they laughed and grimaced with pain. There were fish and birds with sex organs; vicious and transparent animals, tragic and almost human; greedy plants, flowers bearing the pistils and the pustules of sin; a hermaphrodite antelope sniffing cocaine and innocent giraffes grazing on ampoules of morphine; a monkey crushing a phallus between two stones in order to devour the kernel, while his mate, who had her arse stitched up, was trying to undo the knot so as to pleasure herself with the banana she was holding in one paw.

'Dwidwi!' wailed Dan Yack.

He could not bear it any longer. He came out. When he emerged, disorientated, wretched, sad, drunk, infantile, absent-minded and tottering on the threshold of the telephone booth, he was given a huge ovation. The entire cabaret acclaimed his entrance. He was heckled, hooted, cheered. And, as he made no move, the unspeakable Kiki took hold of him by the shoulders and dragged him into a rollicking waltz. Teffi, perched on a table, began to sing (and everyone joined in the chorus):

> *Il se fait taper dans les baguettes*
> *Tous les soirs au fond d'un corridor . . .*[3]

Dan Yack, dominating this outrageous shindy, yelled at the top of his lungs for the *patron* to hear him: 'Pronine! Hey, Pronine! Make some mulled wine, yes, mulled wine for everybody. Salad-bowls, soup-tureens, buckets and basins full of hot wine. All your biggest containers! Fill up a barrel, a bidet. It's my round. I'm not just paying for them to drink, but to get absolutely sozzled!'

And he burst out laughing, then collapsed, exhausted, over a table. And he fell asleep.

And rolled on to the floor.

'Who the hell's this joker snoozing under the table?'

'That's Dan Yack.'

'The millionaire?'

'The famous hell-raiser?'

'The beautiful Hedwiga's lover?'

'The very same.'

'Fine state he's in!'

'What a swine!'

'They say the beautiful Hedwiga's about to leave him.'

'Yes, I heard them talking about it tonight. It seems she's going to marry Ephrim Michaëlovich, you know, the youngest son of old Prince Dobrolioubov, the one who keeps a string of racehorses.'

'What pigs they are, all these rich men,' said Goischman.

The orgy was over. Everyone had gone home. In the shambles of the cabaret, littered with broken glasses, uncountable empty bottles, stained napkins, piles of cigarette-ends and ash, the indefatigable Pronine was chatting with three young men who had just come in. Seated at a round table behind a screen, they were drinking a matinal vodka.

The three young men were Arkadie Goischman, a Jewish poet; Ivan

3   He had himself tossed off/Every night at the end of a corridor . . .

Sabakov, a sturdy peasant from the region of Tambov who was studying at the Academy of Fine Arts; and André Lamont, a puny little St Petersburger of French descent, who was a musician. These three inseparables, after spending the night on the Islands (those long white nights on which the sun never set, when all St Petersburg was out and about, drinking, gossiping, feverishly indulging its vices), after enthusiastically discussing art, aesthetics, philosophy, books, painting in France, Germany, Asia, Italy, England and America all night long, had got into the habit of coming to the cabaret in the early mornings to drink Monopolka with Pronine, and the *patron*, a kindly giant, welcomed them warmly, offering them a first bottle, followed by a big plate of *zakouzkis*, and an infinity of small tots, for Pronine knew they were poor and he was proud to be in a position to oblige artists.

'And to think these are the sort of pigs we have to work for!' added Goischman, the poet.

'Not on your life!' protested Ivan Sabakov. 'Me. I work for Art. I . . .'

'Art, my arse!' Goischman heatedly interrupted him. 'Tell me then, Ivan, is it Art . . . Art, the Academy and Phidias who pay you to stuff your guts, or is it old General Nicolas Linden, who's commissioned you to sculpt his wife's tomb? Christ! Ask André who he works for, ask *him*.'

'Me?' Lamont replied coldly. 'I work for my mistress.'

'Long live Lulu the dressmaker!' Goischman cried triumphantly.

'And why not?' declared André Lamont. 'She pays for my grub when I frighten the life out of her.'

'What's that you're saying?' Sabakov asked anxiously.

André Lamont gulped down a glass of vodka, then explained brazenly: 'Lulu is a very nervous type - what the Germans would call a hysteric. So, when I desperately need money, I pay a visit to her smart boutique. It's full of rich clients, all as crazy as she is, and I play one of those "Nocturnes" that have made me famous, they're full of moonlight, bells and ghosts, and I scare them all stiff. You know Lulu's installed a magnificent Steinway in her fitting-rooms?'

'Does she keep you, then?' Goischman insinuated.

'Sometimes,' Lamont admitted.

'Lulu?'

'Lulu and her clients, and some of her working girls,' said Lamont complacently enumerating his conquests.

'André!' cried the innocent Ivan Sabakov. 'Tell me it's not true, that you're lying! I don't know any creature as pure and disinterested as you are!'

'How naïve these sculptors are!' crowed a jubilant Goischman.

'My God,' declared André Lamont cynically, 'our greatest Russian musician lives with a great Parisian *couturière*. Why shouldn't I do the same here?'

'Especially if she inspires you to works of genius!' added Goischman.

'As to that,' answered Lamont, 'we are even bigger pigs than the rich. Art, and particularly music, serves more than one purpose.'

'Arkadie! André!' protested Sabakov. 'Shut up! You disgust me. If I didn't know you better, I'd . . .'

'But you don't know anything, my little one,' the poet Arkadie Goischman interrupted once again. 'Listen, your friend, your god, Alexander – yes, Alexander Korolenko, the man you've bored our ears off about, the inventor of line, the cube, the sphere, the man who has revitalized modern sculpture, the apostle of pure sculpture, of sur-sculpture, has always had beautiful women. What a flaw in his character! I ask myself, in parenthesis, how an artist, a great artist, can live with a beautiful woman and still produce his work. Isn't art sufficient for him, then? As for your Korolenko, who used to live in Paris with the most beautiful woman in France, I met him recently in New York. He'd just married a German – it seems she's the most beautiful woman in Europe – and he no longer works for anything except dollars. Not content with two mistresses – his wife and his sculpture – he has also found himself a master: the dollar. What a genius!'

'But you yourself, Arkadie, who do you write for?' came the ardent question from Ivan. 'All those beautiful love poems of yours, and those magnificent pages about the poor and unfortunate in the great cities?'

'Me?' said Goischman. 'I work for money. One's got to live, after all.'

'And has your work earned you a lot of money, Monsieur Goischman?' inquired Pronine, much amused by this discussion between the three friends.

'Not a bean,' the poet humbly admitted, 'and that's just what infuriates me. Not even enough to buy myself a smoke! Pronine, give me one of your cigars. Thanks. I'm so broke that I'm becoming a creature of luxury, I can live on nothing but Havanas and, if this goes on, very soon I shan't be able to do without my poverty, it will be like a drug, like opium. The very thought of a beefsteak nauseates me. Even now I can't imagine how I could write those beautiful poems you speak of, my dear Ivan, if my belly wasn't empty. Pronine, pour me another drink!'

'I knew it, I knew it!' exclaimed Ivan, drunk with joy.

'Wait a moment, little one,' said Goischman bitterly. 'Just you wait till I get the chance and you'll see if I don't know how to blow a mint of money . . .'

'You can always prostitute yourself,' André Lamont insinuated in his turn.

'That's what I'm going to do, André, that's what I'm going to do!' shouted the poet.

'And what will you do with your money?' asked Pronine.

'Monsieur,' Arkadie Goischman answered him, 'when a poet like me has as much money as you have, or as this revolting moron who's snoring under our table, I shall no longer write except for the glory of Cimabue's Madonna. I shall go and burn my poems in front of her portrait in Sienna.'

'That's a dirty Jew talking,' murmured Lamont, leaning towards Pronine.

'Arkadie! Arkadie!' cried Sabakov passionately. 'That's splendid, what you just said! Say it again, say it again! You're right, we should all work for the Madonna. From now on, I'm only going to work for St Basil of Mount Athos. Like my father, who painted icons in his village and learned his art from his father. All my work from now on will be in keeping with the tradition.'

'But there's never been any tradition of sculpture in Russia!' jeered André Lamont.

'Perhaps not in St Petersburg,' Ivan Sabakov retorted, 'not in this country of bogs and marshes! But in my village there's an old stone set up by the ancients. It's completely rounded. One would say it was a prehistoric Venus with a fat belly and three breasts. The peasants dance round it on the Eve of St John. Moreover, with us, everybody is a sculptor. Everybody works in wood, and it's in wood that I'm going to work from now on. In oak, the very heart of oak! *O douba, doubina,* O good people of my village, you're going to see me working in the forest, I'm going to carve you a St Basil taller than the steeple of the monastery church! And you, Arkadie, will pose for me, you've got the noble forehead of this great saint, his scornful authority and his compassionate heart for the poor and wretched!'

'Me?' protested Arkadie the poet. 'I don't know how to pose. I can't keep still.'

'And why not?'

'I've never had a home. I wouldn't be able to stop fidgeting.'

'It's the same with me,' said Lamont. 'I compose my music while I'm strolling through the streets, and I write it in brasseries and cafés.'

'I haven't got a studio, either,' said Ivan. 'I work in the open air, in the cemetery as a rule. But I've just rented an abandoned tennis-court. I'll have an old railway-sleeper taken there and you'll come and pose for me, won't you, Arkadie?'

'Dogs, I tell you, they treat us like dogs,' declared Goischman, thumping the table with his fist.

'Or like whores,' said André, bitter-sweet.

'The Neva flows right past my place,' said Ivan dreamily. 'Come on, let's go. I'm going to start work at once. The saint holding himself upright, rigid. His head ten times as big as his belly. My father painted according to the rules, he never worried about proportion.'

'The author of *The Imitation* has already declared', said Goischman, puffing on his cigar, 'that the earth is no bigger than a pin-head.'

'When shall I be able to get back to my own home?' sighed André Lamont, thinking of a quiet room, a harpsichord, a goose-feather quill, a ream of glazed paper. 'I would love to get down to work!'

'And me, too!' said Arkadie Goischman. 'Come on, let's push off. Only the filthy bourgeoisie can afford an ivory tower.'

'Wait, my friends, stay a moment,' Pronine objected. 'Wait, I'm going to get you another bottle.'

Under the table Dan Yack had been awake for several minutes now. He had overheard some fragments of the discussion that was going on right over his head. They reached him as if through a sieve, sifted through the thickness of the table, so that his awakening was, as it were, dredged with a fine wheaten flour of words that had neither head nor tail. What really intrigued him and made him squint were the four pairs of shoes planted close to his head. He screwed in his monocle and examined them closely. There was a little pair of buckskin boots that jigged up and down each time a falsetto voice was raised; Dan Yack imagined this voice as coming from a pasty face pitted with blackheads and cold sores. There were two large, ill-matched boots in fawn leather, down-at-heel, spattered with mud, but impassive and anonymous. There were two patent-leather pumps, crumpled, split, with their laces missing, from whose staved-in uppers emerged a pair of flesh-coloured silk socks. These two pumps rested one on top of the other, and every time an impassioned voice rang out, they trampled on each other, and whenever a fist thudded down and shook the table, the left heel crushed the point of the right toe. Finally, right beside his ear, were the two supple red morocco leather boots, encrusted with blue beads, which Dan Yack recognized as belonging to Pronine. He watched as these two boots disappeared for an instant, to return silently, enormous and menacing, into his field of vision.

Then, with an effort, he called out: 'Pronine, my friend, give me a hand, please. I'm paralysed. There, that's it, thanks,' he added as he surfaced from beneath the table.

Dan Yack settled himself comfortably in an armchair, screwed in his monocle, stared rudely at the three artists, then said: 'It's odd, I don't recognize you. From an examination of your shoes, I had imagined you to be quite different. Excuse me, gentlemen, for having eavesdropped on your conversation. I was lying there under the table and it was quite unintentionally, I assure you, that I overheard part of your discussion. I wouldn't claim to have grasped the whole scope and meaning of it, but I believe all three of you were complaining of being homeless. That's odd because, as from today, I myself am in the same condition, except that, while you are looking for a home, I don't want one any more. You're artists, aren't you? Permit me to introduce myself, you may have heard of me already. I am Dan Yack, the English millionaire all St Peterburg is talking about. Ah well, that life is over, if you see what I mean.'

Dan Yack, who had risen to his feet, sat down again, and taking a cheque book out of his pocket, added: 'Listen, I could give each of you a million roubles.' Then, turning towards the thunderstruck Pronine, he said: 'Bring me something to write with and go and find us a bottle of champagne. Take one from my own bin.'

'It's Roederer *brut grande cuvée*, from my personal reserve,' he explained, turning towards the three young men. 'There's nothing more wholesome to drink in the morning on an empty stomach. You don't know France? What a country!'

During the whole time that Pronine was absent, Dan Yack said not another word. His cheque-book lay open in front of him. He was toying with his monocle.

Suddenly he burst out laughing and chanted the refrain that kept running through his head: . . . *et benedictus fructus ventris tui* . . .

He dived under the table, then came up again, bawling: . . . *Amen!* Swallowing his laughter, he made a frightful grimace and said: 'I wanted to see if those really were your shoes down there!'

Pronine returned, bearing a magnum in triumph. Then he went to find writing materials.

Dan Yack adjusted his monocle, signed the three cheques, emptied his glass at one gulp and went on: 'Look, I've left the amounts blank. You can fill them in and date them to suit yourselves. My signature is valid. I, personally, have between five and seven million pounds sterling, and, since yesterday evening, I am the sole proprietor of the firm of William and William, Shipowners, of Liverpool – capital, twenty-five million pounds. We have a monopoly on the Arctic and Antarctic fisheries and there isn't a bank in the world whose cashiers would refuse to pay you on these scraps of paper, as long as you present them during banking hours. But, if you prefer, you're welcome to tear them up,' added Dan Yack, yawning.

There was a long silence.

Dan Yack wiped his monocle, put it back in his eye, scowled with his left eyebrow to hold it in, smiled foolishly, yawned again and said: 'I beg your pardon, I'm sleepy. But before I go to take a bath, I have another serious proposition to put to you. Pronine, please do me a favour. Go and warn Billy, my manservant, that I shall not be coming back to the house. Tell him to bring my toilet things to the pool at the Club du Turkestan, as well as my No. 3 case, the one with the pearl-grey flannel suit in it. Tell him to come and find me at the baths, and to hire a comfortable, rubber-tyred carriage to take me directly to the station. But, before he does that, he must call in at the Petit Club de la Noblesse, Quai des Anglais, to pick up my walking-stick, the one with the amber knob, which I left behind last night, and tell the old slowcoach to hurry, I don't want to miss today's train.'

When Pronine was already on the doorstep, setting a large Caucasian cap on top of his blue wig, he shouted to him: 'You know where I live? No. 7, the Moika, first floor, on the left. And now to our business, gentlemen,' Dan Yack went on, addressing the three young men. 'Let us be quick, for I am anxious to go and practise the crawl. Are you fed up with the lives you're leading? Me, too! This is what I propose. Today is the 3rd September. On the 17th November, that is to say, in just over two months' time, my 192-ton steam schooner, *The Old William*, will raise anchor at Liverpool, between five and seven in the morning. I shall be on board. Join me there. The *Old William* revictuals our whaling fleets in the southern oceans. *Down there, far south, somewhere between the heel of New Zealand and the South Pole, where ships never venture*, as some ass wrote in *The Times* the other day. Well then, that's where I'm going to take you. Does the idea appeal to you? I'm offering you a voyage round the world and a home for, let's say, one year, on an island which will belong to nobody but ourselves, just the four of us. Expenses for equipment, etc., will be my responsibility. No conditions, except an undertaking from each one of us to let the others live in their own fashion, within the limitations imposed by our island. Do you agree to that? Don't answer immediately, you have time to make up your minds. But, I swear to you, I'm counting on you absolutely for the 17th November. Don't lumber yourselves with luggage, *The Old William* will be fully fitted out to receive you and ensure a comfortable crossing, and I myself will be standing by the gangway, between five and seven a.m., to welcome you aboard. All you need bring, each of you, is the tools of your trade. One last word on the subject and then I'm off. The Northern Express leaves at one minute past noon and waits for no man. You are artists. I must warn you that I am neither a collector, nor a patron, nor an art lover. I understand nothing about art and I always found my Aunt Regula's passion for paintings and antique furniture ridiculous. I've never read a book and I've never understood why they put up statues, which do nothing but hold up the traffic in bustling cities. Music bores me stiff, I don't like anything except the nasal bleating of phonographs and the loud roar of gramophones. I can guarantee to bring a whole cargo of records and cylinders with me, as well as half a dozen of the latest and most highly perfected machines. I shall also bring my dog, Bari. He's a long-haired St Bernard, and, of course, the largest available flask of the fashionable perfume-of-the-moment. And, with that, let me say *au revoir*, my friends, see you soon!'

And Dan Yack ran out of The Stray Dog.

Out in the street, he began to sing.

He was still singing in the swimming-pool as he performed an impeccable overarm stroke.

And when, several hours later, the Northern Express left St Petersburg, Dan Yack was singing in his *wagon-lit*:

et benedictus fructus ventris tui . . .
. . . A-a-a-men!

Three faces, glued to the windows of the station buffet, watched the train pull out.

PART TWO

LONGITUDE 164° 3′ E
(from Greenwich)
LATITUDE 67° 5′ S

On 4th March 1905, the *Green Star*, formerly *The Old William*, which Dan Yack had rebaptized, left Hobart Town and sailed down the Derwent.

It was almost five o'clock in the evening.

The pilot who was taking her out to sea was a colossus who, one day, had taken it into his head to blow out his brains. The bullet had jammed and the explosion had blasted away part of his lower jaw, disfiguring the man's enormous face and leaving a hideous scar; his smile was frightful.

The current carried the schooner rapidly towards Bruni Island, which lay on their starboard bow and could be identified by a gigantic dead tree-trunk. They were now almost level with Rabbit Island, whose lighthouse sends out a beam every fifty-nine seconds.

Once past these islets, one enters Storm Bay, the bay of tempests and, as the pitching and rolling started, the *Green Star* began pouring out dense black smoke which the south-east wind maliciously beat back on to the bays and mountains of Tasmania, as if to blot out her contours.

It is a tricky passage and demands a good pilot.

Bad Bay, rival to Storm Bay, stretches between Tasman Head and Bruni Island. Hugging the coast of Penguin Island, ships make a beeline between Cape Fluted and Cape Frederick Henry; leaving Entrecasteaux Channel to starboard, they pass Cape Raoul, whose curious basalt masses, cut into colonnades, resemble (when seen from a distance) a Greek temple whose walls and roof have collapsed – the Temple of Cape Sunium, for example. Here, the pilot leaves the ship, which sails on into the open sea, leaving in its wake Pedra Blanca, Nossa Senhora do Pilar and Eddystone Rock, the last outposts of Van Diemen's Land.

The setting sun was pale and ghostly. It was cold. An icy breeze was blowing from the South Pole. The thermometer had dropped to two degrees below zero.

Next day, the same cold, the same swell coming from the south; dense fog without a break; no sun at midday and, consequently, no latitude reading.

On the 6th, 7th, 8th, 9th, 10th, 11th and 12th, storms. To these seven days of tempest add thirteen days of navigating through continuous fog, a black and bitter cold and formidable swells, for, in these solitary regions, the waves of the Pacific Ocean roll for a distance of 2,000 leagues, that is to say, from Banks Peninsula as far as the coasts of Chile, without a single island, an islet or a rock emerging to break up the surface.

Winter threatened.

Beneath the wan light of the lamps hung in gimbals, Captain Deene, the commander of the schooner, Dan Yack, Arkadie Goischman, André Lamont and Ivan Sabakov were reunited around the table in the saloon.

The ship's master, Deene, a skinny, weather-beaten little man with a shy manner and a pinched, sorrowful expression, occupied the place of honour. Facing him, at the opposite end of the table, Dan Yack was preparing a punch. His gestures were fastidious. He was wearing a suit of thick blue ratteen, the jacket had wide lapels and was adorned with a double row of gilt buttons. When he turned his head, his monocle glinted below the embroidered peak of a naval officer's cap. A large St Bernard was lying at his feet. To his right, Ivan Sabakov was stretched out on the bench that ran across the bulkhead. He had adopted sailors' garb, the red woollen shirt worn by whalers, trousers made of 'devil's skin' and long rubber boots that came up to his thighs. He was teasing the dog under the table, then, presently, he rested his elbows on the table, his head moving forward into full light as he shook back his long chestnut hair. To his left, sitting astride a chair that he had turned back to front, was Arkadie Goischman, puffing on a slim Sumatra cigar. His hands were clasped together, his eyes closed, his chin resting on the back of the chair. His pale, clean-shaven face, the forehead heightened by incipient baldness, and bitter lines around the mouth, looked as if it were moulded in plaster. Whether from pride or disdain, he was wearing the same dirty, unkempt clothes, several sizes too large for him, that he had been wearing in St Petersburg, and he still flaunted the same cracked patent-leather pumps and the same flesh-coloured socks, which he had refused to discard or change, and in which he had just travelled half-way round the world. At the far end of the cabin, close to the cast-iron stove, stood André Lamont, arrogant and shivering, trying to warm himself. He was extraordinarily elegant. He had on a white linen suit made especially for the voyage; it had a belted jacket and baggy trousers, or rather, knickerbockers. He was proud of his exquisite golfing shoes, purchased in Bombay, and of his crocodile-skin leggings, which he had unearthed in some market-booth in Colombo. He was sporting a yellow cravat with red and green dots. He was chain-smoking, coughing a lot and spitting into a large silk handkerchief that he had pulled out of one of his numerous pockets. A sun-helmet was rammed down on to his skull.

A geographical globe, suspended from the ceiling, hung down between the lamps.

Outside, it was pouring with rain.

Dan Yack spoke.

'I believe,' he said, unfolding a chart amongst the glasses and the small jugs of arrack that cluttered the table, 'I believe it is time to inform our captain of our intentions and to ask his advice. Today, everything depends on him. However, before we hear Captain Deene's opinion, and follow his good counsel which will, I know, be dictated by experience, I would like to remain faithful to the spirit of our escapade and carry it to its logical conclusion. I would like to leave it to Fate to decide the exact location of our sojourn. Let us choose our uninhabited island by pure chance, let it depend on an act of skill, or of clumsiness. You haven't made any choice, have you? Neither have I. That's why I've hung this globe from the ceiling, between the lamps. It is hooked up by its equatorial belt. The part that is most brightly lit, the part facing the door, is the southern hemisphere. Come and stand over here, by the door. Perfect. You see, at three paces, all one can distinguish is a large white patch, in the middle. That's the South Pole. The blue areas are the oceans. At the top, that yellow tongue sticking out is Cape Horn, which we shall round next summer, on our way home. A little lower down, to the right, that brown blob is the Cape of Good Hope, which we rounded three months ago. Lower still, that green emerging from the half-shadows is Australia, which we have only just left behind us. Now, come back to the centre. Look! All around the Pole, in the middle of the white patch of the ice-field, there is a little coronet of land. Also, on the right and higher up, amidst the blur of the ocean, you can see some small dots which are islands. Here's my Browning. Take care! Each of us in turn is going to fire one shot, then Captain Deene will tell us whether the lands we have hit are inhabited, or habitable, and we shall rely on his opinion so as to choose and occupy the most convenient. So, it's a matter of aiming, preferably, for the southern lands or those numerous islets lost in the Atlantic or the Indian Ocean. Don't take the Pole as your bull's-eye, we'll leave the Pole for some future trip, if our association continues and you have the stomach for it. What do you think of my bit of sport, gentlemen? You will have noticed that all the known countries, and Europe, are on the reverse side, in shadow, so there's no danger of hitting them. Who will begin? I propose that the worst shot should fire the first bullet.'

'Me!' said Goischman. 'Give me your gun, I've never held a weapon in my hand, I don't know how it works. I'm utterly indifferent to the whole business, it's all the same to me where I hit. Pity I can't blow up the whole Earth!'

And Goischman closed his eyes as he pulled the trigger.

'Too low, too low!' said Captain Deene, who was acting as referee. 'You have fired much too low, sir. Here, look. This is the spot where your bullet penetrated. Right in the middle of the Antipodes! We passed them, far out to sea, not ten days ago. And look here, look on the other side, run your finger over it. Your bullet has destroyed Paris. Feel the crack? And here's the little bit of plaster that fell off, one can still read . . . *ris*. That's all that's left of *Paris*.'

'Christ!' said Goischman. 'To think I've blown up Paris, that's no joke! Your game is amusing, Dan Yack. What do you say, André, can't you just imagine those fellows in Montmartre with my bullet in their eye?'

'I don't give a damn,' said André. 'Hand me the gun.'

'Excuse me,' said Dan Yack. 'I don't think that shot counts. Those islands are inhabited, aren't they, Captain Deene?'

'Yes,' replied the captain, 'there are half a dozen officials there, who . . .'

'Well then,' said André, 'I'm going to hit the bull's-eye, I'm a crack shot.'

'André,' said Sabakov, 'let me shoot before you do. I've chosen an island in the ocean.'

'Your game is quite absurd, monsieur,' said André Lamont to Dan Yack as he handed the revolver to Ivan.

Sabakov took a long time to aim. He was left-handed. The shot went off, just grazing the sphere of the world.

'Missed!' declared the captain. 'Too far to the right. You must correct your aim. Which island are you aiming at? I believe it was Tristan da Cunha. That is also inhabited. A clergyman and 180 Irishmen. I called there once when . . .'

'Shit!' murmured André Lamont between his teeth.

He took the weapon and fired at random.

The Earth smashed down on to the table and the St Bernard fled in terror.

André Lamont laughed till the tears were pouring down his cheeks. His bullet had cut the string on which the globe was suspended.

'You did that on purpose, monsieur,' Dan Yack protested.

'Well of course I did it on purpose, I told you I was going to hit the bull's-eye! It's as easy as sucking eggs, you know.'

And Lamont poured himself a large glass of punch.

Dan Yack was mortified and, so as to restrain himself from accusing Lamont of cheating, he went out on deck, whistling for his dog.

'What a cretin!' André snarled.

And he lit another cigarette.

Out on deck, it was raining.

'Goddam it!' Dan Yack swore, unable to light his pipe.

He decided to join his dog, who had already settled down in his niche behind the chart-house.

It was not even possible for Dan Yack to take a stroll on the deck of the little ship.

At the foot of each mast a pile of coal reached up to the yards. Packing-cases and casks littered the deck, leaving not a single free passage, and the large sections of a portable cabin, which they had been unable to lower into the hold, had been stowed on deck, wherever they could be fitted in according to their shape and dimensions. Now the whole thing, knotted and fastened together with a network of cords, chains and ropes that crossed and recrossed each other at every level, formed an impenetrable barrier. Dan Yack almost came a cropper; a sudden lurch of the ship knocked him off balance and sent him rolling against the big longboat which filled nearly the whole of the ship's bow, then the pitching sent him head first into the deck-house. At last, he reached Bari's kennel and sat astride its roof.

The night was dense and cold. The *Green Star* shuddered heavily in the darkness. Even the glow of the navigation light on the mainmast looked bleary under the eyelid of the fog. A long swell, like an invisible snake whose whitish scales Dan Yack glimpsed from time to time, treacherously entwined itself about the vessel. To port and starboard, the incessant, plaintive cries of penguins rang out. Other birds sobbed in the wind. The engine thumped dully, groaned, rattled unceasingly. The drenched sails flapped and chattered.

Dan Yack was furious at not seeing an outcome to his game. It had been a total failure. He felt that someone had robbed him of a pleasure. And he had been so proud of his bit of sport! The idea had come to him in London, when he was in his company offices, making all the necessary arrangements for a long absence. He had got up immediately and gone out, leaving his managing director in the lurch. A quarter of an hour later he was in the Army and Navy Stores, where he bought a large terrestrial globe. There were hundreds of globes in the shop. He would never have believed there could be so many.

'What it comes down to,' he said to himself, 'is that I'm angry because I'd already chosen my island and was sure of my shot, angry because they didn't give me a chance to fire, angry because I'd imagined that those fellows wouldn't have a clue how to handle a firearm, and because that little what's-his-name? André? André Lamont is very clever, and, above all, I'm angry because I was counting on a clumsy shot by one or other of us to force us into doing something really extraordinary that would send us all to the devil. It's tremendously exciting to have chance against you, and that wretched little musician wrecked everything with his skilful shot. Prowess, bah! He might just as well have fired at the lamps. Then we might at least have had a splendid fire on board. What it comes down to is, I'm sulking, sulking like I used to when I was a little boy,' thought Dan Yack.

And this thought made him laugh.

He started playing with his monocle.

He played with it for a long time.

And from time to time he stopped to say to himself: 'I must find some other way, I *must*.'

And he racked his brains, sitting with his legs dangling and his head in his hands.

'Eight bells!' the first mate, who was the officer on watch, suddenly shouted. And the ship's boy struck the bell eight times for midnight.

'Aren't you coming, Bari?' said Dan Yack to his dog. 'It's time to settle down in one's own berth. No? Well then, good-night, old chap, I'm going below.'

And, as he made his way to his cabin, 'What rotten luck, today,' he murmured. 'Nothing's gone right.'

Back in his cabin he wound up a gramophone, reeled off several dozen records and finally went to sleep.

Early next morning Dan Yack was sitting in his bathtub when Captain Deene came into his cabin. Deene had to wait awhile before he could get a word in because a little nasal phonograph was filling the narrow cabin with a young, charmingly artificial female voice. Dan Yack swore that it was a buxom little blonde, wiggling her hips as she sang.

'I can just see her bare legs, Captain. There are little folds above her knees. She's wearing tartan slippers and tapping her heels like this and like that. The others, her pals, who aren't singing but who are there all the same, inside the machine, are all knock-kneed and they're jigging up and down on the stage behind the singer. Do you hear that rhythm?'

> Non, je ne marche pas,
> Non, je ne marche pas,
> J'suis la petite Nana du Canada-a-ah-â!

'Sir,' the captain began determinedly, 'I . . .'

'Wait,' said Dan Yack, 'let me change the cylinder. It's amazing, you'll see. We're leaving the *Folies Bergère* and going into the Tiergarten. Listen:

> Fischerin die Kleine,
> Zeig' mir deine Beine,
> Zeig' mir was dazwischen ist
> Oder ich erwürge dich![4]

'Can you see the old tart who's singing now, Captain?' Dan Yack

4   Little fisher-girl,
           Show me your legs,
           Show me what's between them
           Or I'll throttle you!

exclaimed. 'She's wiggling her fat arse and her triple chin. The sweat's rolling down from under her ridiculous wig. She's holding her skirt between two fingers, hoisting it up and casting saucy looks at her plump round thigh. She's wearing thick blue stockings with garters at the knee. I adore that! What a marvellous invention! Is that ingenious enough for you? Wait a minute, I'm going to let you listen to the cries of a sea-lion that's having its throat cut. Dumfries, your colleague in *The Young William*, now christened *The Black Star*, recorded this for me on the rocks at Wrangel. You remember that famous affair of the 60,000 seals that were clubbed and skinned under the very nose of the Russian patrol vessel? But, as you will hear, they kicked up a hell of a racket. One can only suppose that Dumfries had drugged the entire Russian crew! Incidentally, Captain, why have you never recorded anything for me on your cruises?'

'Dan Yack William, sir,' the captain began, 'I . . .'

'Dan Yack, Dan Yack, short and sweet!' yelled Dan Yack, interrupting him. 'Don't you realize that old Carlos is dead and that I've changed the names of all my ships? There are no more Williams nowadays. I've changed my life, my name, my family, my country, everything!'

'But Mr Yack, I . . .'

'No more mister, no more milord,' cried Dan Yack, prancing with rage in his tub. 'My name is Dan Yack! Dan Yack! Dan Yack!'

Although he was stark naked, he appeared enormous, deformed, bloated and metamorphosed in the swirling steam from the hot tub. Deene, believing he had suddenly been stricken with myopia and presbyopia, rubbed his eyes. His interlocutor seemed unreal, he couldn't get a grip on him. Now crouching down, now standing up, pirouetting, Dan Yack rubbed himself down, poured jugs of water over his head, stretched out his arms, flexed his knees, leapt about, slithered, dripping wet, across the cabin, splashing, foaming, steaming, full of soap and life. He uncorked bottles, wound up the phonograph, flagellated himself with a Turkish towel, put on another record, shampooed his hair.

Finally, he pressed a little spring.

Dan Yack smiled at himself as he looked into a convex magnifying mirror which reflected his animal eye.

Without the monocle.

Deene was embarrassed.

He said nothing.

With a towel round his loins, Dan Yack was shaving.

In the silence one could hear the razor scraping through the hairs, then the click of the gramophone, then a deafening rumble and suddenly a frightful scream that filled the cabin. It was the sea-lion having its throat cut. Its cry rose to a crescendo. Then there was the far-off barking of a million seals, followed by a long moan. Next, the voice of a man shouting at the top of his lungs: 'Kill it, John! Kill it!' A gunshot. Then no more. Then, once again, the baying, but retreating farther and farther into the distance. And, finally, the hoarse sound of a ship's siren.

Or perhaps it was the beast's death-cry.

Dan Yack had stepped back into his tub. A smell of vetiver wafted through the cabin. The needle, at the end of its track, scratched and fretted. On the floor, a pair of nail-clippers glinted.

'Ah, there they are,' cried Dan Yack, 'I've found them!'

And he turned round.

'Captain,' he said. 'Captain, I should like to know if we . . .'

But Deene had gone.

For several days now, ice-floes and icebergs had been drifitng past. The *Green Star* was beating up to windward.

This morning the weather was fine.

The surface of the sea was mottled white with ice-floes and growlers and large stretches of the water were already in the grip of a light and brittle pack-ice. Nevertheless, the undulations of the swell could still be felt. In the wake of the ship the water looked black. There was a fresh wind blowing. Full sail had been set to lighten the burden on the engines.

It was already near midday when Dan Yack appeared on deck. His dog lumbered heavily towards him and almost knocked him over as he rubbed his muzzle against his legs.

'Be quiet, Bari, that's enough. Yes, yes, you're a good old boy, but that's enough now.'

A sliver of blue sky had appeared. Deene was sitting on a bench, waiting for a ray of sunlight. He was holding his sextant at the ready. The crew, keeping a respectful silence, were gathered round him. Ivan Sabakov had joined the circle.

André Lamont, his lips cracked and peeling, was feverishly writing something on his knees. He was leaning back against the longboat, his body swaddled in a blanket from his bunk.

He was coughing.

Dan Yack approached Arkadie Goischman, who was wedged in between two crates, reading.

'What are you reading, Goischman?'

'Here, see for yourself.'

Dan Yack took the book and read the title: *On the Discovery of the Constant Relation between Appearance and Disappearance, Work and Rest, the Minimum and Maximum Extent of the Webs and Attaching-threads of Spiders of different Species, and Atmospheric Variations, 1795.*

'My God, what the hell is this?' Dan Yack asked Goischman, looking at him over the top of the book.

'Poems,' replied Goischman.

'Yours?' asked Dan Yack.

'Oh no, they're by a man called Quatremère-Disjonval, who died more than a hundred years ago.'

'And does all this rigmarole signify something?' Dan Yack persisted.

'It's the story of a man who was condemned to twenty-five years in prison. To sweeten the bitterness of captivity, he devoted himself to the study and observation of various subjects. The style is bizarre, full of paradoxes and piquant and ingenious ideas. There are also some genuine discoveries, including the relation between spiders and hygrometry.'

'How amusing,' said Dan Yack. 'And do you have many books of this sort, Monsieur Goischman?'

'I bought several crates of books, a job lot, on my way through Amsterdam,' replied Goischman.

'I really must read a book some day,' said Dan Yack with a broad smile. 'I wonder if it's as amusing as my phonograph? Certainly your book conjures up a picture of this man, who died such a long time ago, surrounded by spiders that tell him whether the weather is good or bad. That's fascinating! But why should he be interested in fine weather, since he could never leave his cell?'

'Well, good God,' Goischman answered, 'it was a distraction, like any other.'

'Yes, yes, I understand, and I'm sure you're right. Here, Monsieur Goischman,' said Dan Yack, handing back the book, 'one of these days I must play you my record of the sea-lion and you must lend me this book. I'll have a go at reading, down there, but, you know, there aren't even any spiders on our island.'

And Dan Yack went back to the captain.

The bearings had been taken.

'Well?' asked Dan Yack.

'We're tacking sixty-five degrees latitude south and a hundred and sixty-five degrees longitude east,' Deene replied.

'Which means?'

'Which means we are almost there,' the captain affirmed. 'This is an extraordinary year, never before have I sailed into these latitudes without encountering pack-ice.'

'So much the better,' said Dan Yack.

'It will be a terrible winter,' the captain added.

'So?'

'Everyone is of the opinion that, by this evening, we shall be within sight of the pack-ice. You see that yellowish haze on the horizon? That's the ice-field.'

'So?'

'So we shall have to wait till tomorrow morning to search for an open channel.'

'And do you think we shall find one?'

'There's a very good chance that we shall. After all the bad weather we've had, and these latest storms, the pack-ice must be in smithereens. And as long as this wind from the south-east doesn't drop, we shall be able to get through. And provided this lull in the weather lasts.'

'What does the barometer say?'

'Set fair, but that doesn't mean a thing in these regions.'

'And beyond, do you think we shall find open water?'

'Oh, well,' the captain answered, 'one never knows. The season is well advanced, and I believe this must be the first time a ship has still been navigating in these waters at this time of year. Generally, they head north and keep to latitudes a good ten degrees lower. It won't do to hang about on the island. A storm, a shift in the wind and the sea can freeze over in a single night. And then God help you, you've had it.'

'When do you think we might arrive?'

'In four or five days, if we find open water.'

'And if there isn't any?'

'Then never, for I'd never venture into the pack-ice in such

conditions. I don't want to run the risk of the ship getting trapped in
the ice.'

'And what news is there from the whalers on Macquarie?'

'They say there's open water as far as Victoria Land.'

'Well, then?'

'That's just what's worrying me. There's an old saying: "Blue
water, bitter winter".'

'Those men belong to the Compañia Gonzalo Hortalez, don't they?'

'Yes.'

'Well, then, do you trust them?'

'Of course. It's normal practice for sailors to pass this sort of
information among themselves. We take no part in the rivalry
between the ships' owners.'

'So, what is it that's worrying you?'

'This fine weather. It's not natural at this time of year.'

'You are hard to please, Captain.'

And Dan Yack added, bursting into laughter: 'What you need is a
few spiders.'

'What?'

'Lads!' shouted Dan Yack, addressing the crew, who had been
following this exchange, 'a hundred pounds to every man jack of you
if you disembark us at Balleny within a week!'

'Long live Dan Yack!' roared the crew.

'And from tomorrow, Captain, triple rations of rum! Long live the
Green Star!'

'Hurray!' responded the crew, throwing their caps in the air.

The captain shrugged his shoulders and disappeared into his cabin.

He was uneasy.

'Lousy bloody job!' he growled.

The *Green Star* had just got under way.

She was carrying sail so as to escape as swiftly as possible from this
desolate land. There was a hurricane in the offing.

Captain Deene checked the steam-pressure. Cupping his hands
into a megaphone, he shouted: 'Are you ready? How many?'

'Eleven,' replied somebody from the engine-room.

With one eye on the sails, Deene bullied his men.

The captain was in a foul mood.

The crew were not work-shy, but their minds were not on the job.

As they took a reef in the mainsail, the men were thinking of Dan Yack and his three companions, who had disembarked. They were asking themselves: 'What the hell do Three-Eyes and those other jokers hope to find on their island?'

And everyone looked towards the land.

There was no one on the shore except Bari, who was standing at the end of the promontory, barking.

'There's something fishy behind all this,' concluded an old quartermaster as he gave a couple of blasts on his whistle and spat out the juice from his quid of tobacco.

The ship was making heavy weather. They were luffing and steering as close to the wind as possible, so as to bear away from some of the islands. The wind was barely manageable. The pack-ice boomed louder and louder as they approached. They would have to run the gauntlet to get out.

Once more, Deene pointed his telescope at the island. It was getting dark in the bay. The corrugated-iron roof of the portable cabin gleamed, brand new. There was no one on the beach of Balleny except for a little white dot that could be seen climbing the cliff-top path. It was Bari, slowly going back.

Lightning glanced off the coast. Storm-clouds were gathering swiftly. Then, everything became swirling confusion.

'God's thunder!' Deene, caught in the squall, cursed. 'I hope to Christ we can get out of this tonight! But I'm afraid we won't make it!'

Dan Yack was stowing his belongings in his berth. Ivan Sabakov was lighting the lamps. André Lamont and Arkadie Goischman had gone to bed, glum and depressed. Bari was licking the plates. Outside, the storm raged. A sheet of corrugated iron was ripped from the roof. Then a pile of barrels came crashing against the door. The wind besieged the house.

It raged for many days and nights.

The first blizzard.

A white-out.

Winter.

PART THREE

OVERWINTERING

Naturally, things did not run smoothly.

The house, erected in the shelter of the cliff on Sturge Island, the principal islet of Balleny – the one the seal-hunters who frequented these regions in earlier days, during the brief austral summer, had nicknamed The Louse (no one knows why, perhaps on account of its humpbacked shape, its tripartite structure, its ice-cap or its volcanic peak, Mount Brown) – consisted of three sections.

It was a low, elongated building.

The door was at one end. The entrance, a dark hole, contained all the fuel: coal for heating the house during the eight months of winter and drums of paraffin to feed the six large lamps during the night, including the one long night that would last nearly sixty-five days. At the other end was the provision store: crates of biscuits, canned and preserved foods, casks of bacon and sauerkraut, barrels of salted butter, beans, peas, pasta; sacks of flour, rice, tea, sugar loaves, tubs of jam, boxes of chocolates, demijohns of brandy; bales of spare clothing, blankets, furs, cooking utensils, arms and ammunition. The central section, the communal living quarters, was big enough to provide lodgings for an entire crew, but too enclosed for four men.

The stove was set in the middle of the large room. There were four deal tables. Four chairs. Four bunks. Four sets of shelving. Four lamps. Each corner of the room formed, in effect, a cell for a single person, who could use it as his own home, to meditate, think, live, read, write, sleep and digest in isolation behind a partition of tarred sailcloth that hung from a curtain-rod. The only things they held in common were the four leather chairs placed around the stove (four squat, upholstered armchairs that bulged like hunchbacked monsters), the big table (which was pushed against the window during the daytime), two hurricane-lamps, the weapon-rack and the pegs for hats and coats, which were ranged to the right and left of the door.

Cooking was done on a Primus stove.

Each man had his folding aluminium mess tin, his plate, his spoon and his drinking-mug.

Each possessed a good sharp knife.

There was not a single instrument for measuring time; not even a watch to remind them of the passing hours.

And so the time was long, which is its true nature, and, although there was a great deal of dreaming in this house, there was no sleep.

It was André Lamont who destroyed the watches.

Barely a month had passed when he found he could no longer contain himself. He slept fitfully, turning over and over in his bunk. He was bathed in sweat and shivered incessantly. He sat up, draping the covers over his head like a monk's cowl. He listened.

He could hear the wind tearing at the roof and a thousand inhuman breaths straying through the corrugations of the sheet metal, as if through organ-pipes and winding their way out again in corkscrew spirals. But with such violence! The windpipes, the vocal cords were torn, and a solitary voice dropped into a pocket of silence like a severed head into a basket of sound. Stammerings. What is that word which has not been spoken, and who is it making efforts to speak? Day after day, hour after hour, the door vibrated like an overstretched drum-skin, or again, a million soft little tongues came to die, licking and whimpering at the window.

The chimney roared.

The frost tightened its creaking vice. Unseen cracks widened by a hair's breadth. The subsoil. The heart of the cliff. The sea. The sky. The marrow in men's bones. The table. It took a hatchet to cut the bread and a pair of rubber gloves to hold a pen. The very paper became brittle, like flaky pastry.

A clash of cymbals.

André Lamont raised his head. It was the moon, sliding on to the window-pane like a child's 'transfer'. A diamond cutting through space. Pinpoints of light transfixed the coldness. Rimed rivets upheld the sky, monochrome and frosted like a vast crystal. The cold receded into the immensity of space. A thermometer snapped in half. The flame of the lamps burned with a purer light.

In the silence Bari could be heard scratching himself and taking a brief turn about the room. Going up to André, he would sniff at him,

wag his tail and then go back and flop down in front of the fire. Or
sometimes it was Sabakov who leapt nimbly out of his cell to poke the
fire or put on more fuel. Then there would be the clatter of coal, the
rattle of the shovel and the poker, the emptying of the ash-pan with a
rasp like the sound of coughing. When he finished, André Lamont
began coughing in his turn. The fit shattered him. He fell back on to
his bunk.

The kettle whistled.

André worked on his symphony.

Often he wept.

His feet were cold.

He felt a draught as fine as a cheese-wire cutting into his lungs.

He started coughing again.

When the fit was over, he heard a cracking sound. It was Arkadie
Goischman lighting a cigar in his corner.

'Hey, Arkadie, aren't you asleep?'

Arkadie did not answer. Arkadie never answered. The red glow of
his cigar burned for a long time, extinguishing itself or intensifying
like a lens with a shutter.

André could hear the approaching footsteps of the mammoth of the
mists. A hairy, maned beast came to scratch its back against the
house. Its breathing was like a pair of bellows and its breath fouled the
air. André heard its glottis move as it swallowed. Intestinal rumblings.
The heavy brute slept on its feet. It sweated, then it froze to the spot,
opaque, solid. Never, never again would they be able to go out. It was a
house of the dead.

'André, André, come on, it's time to eat!'

They told him it was daytime. But it was always night, without the
faintest glimmer of light. He got up. He ate. He went back into his
corner. He came out again to eat. He began to write once more. He
refused to help with the chores. 'Water? What for? We don't need
water!' And he would not go out. He smoked cigarettes. He worked.
The blood rushed to his head. Tears, droplets of sweat fell on to the
staves. He inked them in with Indian ink. Natural, B flat, key of C.
F sharp. He had a fever. He worked on his symphony. He fell asleep,
exhausted. He woke up with a start. His ears were ringing. He thought
he could hear church-bells.

It was Dan Yack winding up one of his gramophones.

'Ah! that fellow . . .'

Then he thought about Lulu, his little *couturière*.

He missed his usual audience.

No women! And little by little he began to feel afraid.

Arkadie Goischman was not working. Nevertheless, he did not move around very much. He was ruminating. From time to time he would go to fetch ice or snow, for he was still washing himself although he had given up shaving. His beard was growing high up on his cheeks and becoming very, very long. It was a splendidly Semitic beard.

He had also developed a tic that was becoming a mania. He repeatedly lifted his left hand to his face, scratched his nose, pinched it between thumb and index finger, and then set to pulling at it to make it longer.

With his right hand Goischman never let go of his cigar. He was ruminating. He had grown very fat. His face was bloated. And, as he was becoming visibly balder, he had taken to knotting a chequered handkerchief over his cranium. His motionless shadow, thrown on to the partition screen, was a bizarre Negro's head, with the four knots of the handkerchief and his elongated nose, the nose that he pulled at incessantly. And his hand and arm cast a shadow like an elephant's trunk on the wall. His corner, then, was filled with this enormous bulk that rarely moved and which was perforated by an eye. A glowing eye. The eye of the cigar. Arkadie Goischman was ruminating.

He was the victim of a psychic phenomenon to which the most cultivated as well as the crudest of creatures - a scholarly bacteriologist no less than a rough sailor - quite commonly succumbs during the long polar night. This malady is most difficult to combat. Suddenly, without rhyme or reason, in the middle of an occupation which may be absorbing all your attention and demanding all your presence of mind, you are distracted by an image of some kind which rises in your consciousness and imposes itself on you with an intensity, an appearance of reality and a minuteness of detail which are almost painful. It is generally a scene from your past, your home, and almost always a scene of family life, whether recent or long past. Not only are you incapable of dragging your eyes away from it, but you are actually there, with your loved ones. You turn the pages of a book you read as a child, you sit on your mother's lap, you recall the sound of her voice, and you hear a word, an inflection, a sigh, which brings you back to yourself. This kind of double vision lasts only a few seconds and you soon regain contact with the reality around you. But it can easily cast a shadow over a mind inclined to melancholy.

What made Arkadie Goischman's case peculiar was that the poet had nothing else to do, nothing other than inducing these unexpected returns to the past, taking pleasure in them and having no wish to detach himself from them. He could no longer master them, because, never having had a home or having known his family, he had to struggle to recognize the faces that came to haunt him, and his attention focused anxiously on the search for a name, a proper name, just one, a family name, his own, which he could set up as a dyke against the tumultuous flood of associations, of images and faces, which carried him away. His efforts were in vain. His past, like his life, was in shreds. There was nothing but scraps, rags and tatters. O miserable vagabondage! Unutterable solitude.

Endless night.

Thus, he saw himself in a little neighbourhood café. In which town? He did not know. It must have been winter, for the old, bearded men who were questioning him wore furs. He was very small, tiny in their midst. He was uneasy. They were asking him who he was, the names of his parents, his own name, and he didn't know and he was crying, with his little hands over his eyes. He might have been four or five years old. Suddenly a violent slap sent him rolling under the tables. The old men were fighting amongst themselves. He could hear their shrill, high-pitched voices. In what language were they quarrelling, and where did this scene take place? The only thing Goischman could say for certain was that he was just an infant at the time and that he was always hungry. Desperately hungry.

As he sought to place this scene and discover the reason for his presence among the old men, he kept pulling intermittently at his nose. Hunger loomed so large in his recollections! And it was this sensation of hunger that brought him back to himself. He opened his eyes and lit another cigar.

Arkadie Goischman, thanks to the munificence of Dan Yack, had a supply of cigars within reach of his hand, cigars from Sumatra, which he himself had bought at Padang when the *Green Star* put in there. The shop was run by some kind of Swiss or Hamburger or Dutch woman. She had had one eye missing. With a hideous smile she had invited him into the back of the shop for a drink. From this back room came monosyllabic cries, as if from an aviary, and the eyes of many women glittered from the rush matting as if glass beads had been scattered from a broken necklace. Goischman made his escape, for he

was still a virgin, but he was almost certain he had caught a glimpse of
André Lamont making love with six little native girls.

Goischman pulled his nose. He looked about him. Bari was there,
barking. Lamont was at his table, writing. Ivan was sitting up in bed,
eating beans. Dan Yack was freshening the air in the room with a little
spray.

Arkadie dragged on his cigar and let out a huge puff of blue smoke.
He watched it drift.

The room is full of smoke. He is in New York. He has just finished
speaking at a meeting. As he comes down from the platform, a voluble
Jewish garment-worker grabs hold of him and drags him out into the
street, railing against the foreman, who debauches the seamstresses
in the workshops. He gesticulates a lot, his voice is hoarse; but what is
his name and why are they sitting together on a bench in a square?
This must be Union Square, or isn't it, rather, somewhere in
Brooklyn, or at the end of the Bowery, opposite the Jew's Follies? He
doesn't know any more.

Goischman kept pulling his nose. He turned his back towards the
partition. His cigar had gone out. He chewed the end of it. They called
him. He did not answer. He could not answer. He was struggling to
find out where he was and why he was there. Yes, why?

He is stark naked in front of a mirror. He is at least ten years old and
it is a feast-day, for all the candles in the room are lit and, the evening
before, they killed a goose. He is standing on top of a chest of drawers
in front of a mirror and he dare not move for fear of upsetting a bottle
of eau-de-Cologne between his feet. A woman of about forty is
combing her hair in front of him. It is this woman who has undressed
him, washed him and set him naked on the chest in front of the mirror
(the wallpaper in the room is patterned with big bouquets of garnet-
red roses). She has long black hair. She must be an old maid, he thinks,
because she is not wearing a wig like a married woman. He has a vague
idea that she is his aunt, or a distant relative of his aunt, or a long-lost
friend of the family. There is a link somewhere, very tenuous, but
sufficient to bring them together in this illuminated room. Her name
is . . . but what is her name? Bella . . . or Léna . . . or Mi . . . or No .
. . ? She is pressing herself against him. Her complexion is greasy. Her
forehead smells of hazel-nut oil. But what is she doing? God, what
does she want from him? He cries out. He runs away. He tumbles into
a kitchen full of people. They are celebrating a marriage there. They
throw him out. And after him, his trousers. Then his shirt.

'Dirty goy!' they shout.

Is that, perhaps, why they call me Goischman? he wondered now in anguish. Am I not Jewish, then? All this happened a long time ago, somewhere in a Jewish village in Galicia, somewhere near Wyszenska in Polish Switzerland. But what was the name of those people who never gave me back my boots, and why was I with them? And what did she want from me? That No . . . or Mi . . . or Léna . . . or Bella . . . what did she want? Yes, what?

He pulled his nose.

For a long time.

He was searching.

Searching for a subject for a novel. Yes, that was it.

I must find some link of kinship between all the people I met during my vagabond life. The doss-houses, the farms and châteaux, the emigrants down in the hold, the tarts in the cafés, the anarchists, the rich men. Bastards from every country who will become just one big family and whose history I shall relate.

Eleven thousand faces haunt him. His family.

He is going to write the novel of his life. He is going to recount his life story. That's it. His poems are nothing but lies. Now, at last, he is going to tell his story. The truth. Everything he can imagine about other people, how he met them and why they have become part of his heart, his memory, his innermost being. He doesn't want to be alone in the world any more.

Ah!

Brotherhood.

He falls asleep. At peace.

When he wakes up, he speaks for the first time in forty days: 'André, I'm going to follow your example, could you let me have an exercise book with white paper?'

As he is making this request, his eye lights on Dan Yack.

'Incidentally, what am I to make of that one? He's an enemy . . .'

He begins to dream again.

He comes to himself.

He has no desire to go out any more.

He gives up smoking and no longer washes.

Ivan Sabakov moved around a great deal. He was perpetually coming and going. He felt a need to occupy himself. He had cheerfully taken on the coal fatigue and he put his heart into the task of keeping up a good fire. Every now and then he went outside.

In spite of this, he could not sleep. So he ate. He ate ten, twenty, thirty times a day, apart from the meals prepared by Dan Yack. He always kept a layer of fat at the bottom of his mess tin, a kind of frozen jelly which melted rapidly on the stove; to this he would add a sachet of cocoa or a bouillon cube, macaroni, coffee, sugar, salt, a dollop of lard, a pinch of tea, a good handful of haricot beans or a ship's biscuit. He swallowed this scalding-hot beverage, indifferent to the strong smell of paraffin it gave off. Often there were shreds of tobacco in it, or the dottle of a pipe. He ate it all up. Never had Ivan felt so fit. He always had a hearty appetite.

Ivan had found a wonderful occupation: polishing the lamps.

Sitting in one of the armchairs in the centre of the room, he would hold a lamp between his knees. The lamp was large, round, bulbous and made of copper. Ivan rubbed it with rotten-stone, then he buffed it for a long time with jeweller's rouge and finally, armed with a chamois leather, he burnished it till it glistened and shone. He could never get enough of it. He was dedicated to his task.

Oh, dear God, he thought gratefully, how beautiful the world is!

He went to fetch the sketch-book he had always kept by him on board the *Green Star*. He flicked through the pages. All his designs, all his drawings, all his quick sketches bespoke a youthful insolence. What confidence in life! Heightened by just a few light touches of water-colour, all these pages were matutinal. His subjects were stretching themselves, yawning, smiling, waking up. They were coming to life for the first time. A sailor, smoking his pipe and leaning back against the mainmast with the air of a world conqueror. A nautch-girl dancing, rosy and iridescent. A Negress, pregnant, heavy, rotund, her buttocks daubed with sunlight, the very personification of a bush-goddess. A sailor's dance with a celestial accordion in the foreground that was laughing with all its keys, all its teeth. And more young women and girls from Ceylon or Sumatra, light and voluptuous like the stylized vegetation of their countries. Then pages and pages of children, too healthy, too rich not to be in rags, smiling little Negroes, smiling little Malays, smiling little Hindus, black, coppery, red, brown, yellow children, baked and rebaked by the sun, half-breeds, extraordinary offspring of that synthetic sperm the White Man sows in all his ports of call, flotsam from the luxuriant beaches, the laughingly offered garlands, the wild acclamations that greet every ship which touches port, a great living banner that the native women have run up on the shores of all the oceans of the globe to embellish the civilization of heavy industry which is advancing on them and wants to disembark; the divine children of insouciance.

Ivan picked up another lamp, started polishing again and lost himself in a confused dream of the future, of happiness and joy in living.

He was a miner in the depths of his mine. Tons of minerals were piling up on the earth's surface. Armed with a giant shovel and an enormous poker, he was stoking a glowing furnace in which the four elements of the universe were being consumed. He made himself a hammer, a chisel, tools. He attacked an immense pyramid-shaped mountain, volcanic, basaltic, hard and black, whose stone resounded beneath his blows like a phonolite; every splinter that flew off was square. What exhausting work! He had to hammer away at it a million times before he succeeded in drawing forth a shoulder, a supple neck, the small of a back, a leg, from crutch to heel, a rounded ankle, a streamlined form. The base of his monument was composed of a seething mass of Cyclopean beings and, from out of this mêlée, men, walking upright, escaped to climb the first stage of the mountain. In their muscular arms they clasped women of all races. The women sprouted gaily from these embraces, laughing, delicate, startled; like a swarm of butterflies or birds they flitted round the mountain in a spiral and almost reached the summit. But this summit was ventricose. A cloud of chubby children clung to it, boys and girls who sang as they circled round. In the middle of the circle an adolescent boy sat alone. He stood up. Gradually mounting upward, he moved round the highest peak. Step by step he climbed up, now facing front, now in profile, now with his back turned. Ever higher and higher. At last he took off alone into the void. He had reached the summit. A ball, a sphere, a globe, the earth, a lamp, the sun, which he tried to wrench free, striving to lift it and hold it up, high, very high, in the air, at arm's length, without weakening. Prometheus!

I am going to sculpt the lightning! thought Ivan Sabakov.

He needed a model for his young god. The most beautiful male nude in a multitude of poses.

'I can't pose myself, even though I'm by far the youngest,' Ivan said to himself.

'How vast the world is!'

Bari had just drawn him out of his reverie by rubbing against him.

Sabakov got up, stood on tiptoe to reach the hook. He hung the lamp
back in its place. He lit it. His face was illuminated from above. He
smiled, as happy and as proud as an Olympian. Then he took his mess
tin off the stove and fell to eating with a hearty appetite. He needed
some nourishment.

Beans, like a Greek shepherd, he thought.

He threw a mouthful to the dog.

He looked about him.

In the corner, André Lamont, thin and convulsed like a doomed
man, was working on his symphony. There were moments when he
appeared to be flying on some invisible and inaudible instrument, his
feet working the pedals while, simultaneously, he himself was swung
to and fro, in tempo, like a pendulum or a metronome, carried beyond
space and time. In the opposite corner, Goischman, motionless,
ungainly, thickset and as mangy as a caged beast, gnawed his
penholder furiously as if it were the bars of his cage. His eyes were
pocked with ink-stains, like his fingers, his table, his paper, the floor
of his bolt-hole. How impotent he was! He had not yet written a line.

Ivan Sabakov began to observe Dan Yack.

'Yes,' he said to himself, 'this fellow will do me nicely. All his
movements are precise. How handsome he is! Only a Chinaman or an
Englishman could be so at ease in the world. But why does he wear
that disfiguring monocle?'

And Ivan continued to study Dan Yack.

At the same time, without his being aware of it, he began to
succumb to his influence.

For example, when he went outside, he dressed himself with
meticulous care.

When he went out to search the environs of the cabin, to find and
decide upon which mountain he would use to sculpt his great work as
soon as the sun appeared, Ivan Sabakov wore his anorak with all the
grace and coquetry of a young Russian peasant.

Bari was sad.

Why?

Although he loved his master, Bari detested going out and had a
horror of the cold. There was still another reason why he was
becoming estranged from Dan Yack. Dan Yack reminded him of
England and of all the comforts that he, as a dog, appreciated: the big

lawn where he went to relieve himself, the sunny flight of steps from
which he could so conveniently keep one eye on the gate, the peaceful
house he had made his home, the flunkey who brought him copious
platefuls of scraps, the thick carpet in the little drawing-room where
he usually took his afternoon nap, and Mrs Darwin, the housekeeper,
who petted him and fed him toast at five o'clock, buttered toast spread
with gooseberry jam. All this now came back to him dimly while Dan
Yack was calling him, and he caught the strong odour of that vetiver
which tickled his nose and in whose scent he rediscovered the perfume
of the good, leisurely life in that tranquil country which, until recently,
had been his beautifully waxed and polished kingdom. That was
why Dan Yack gave him the hump. At the first opportunity he would
go back, lie down in front of the fire and close his eyes, even though he
could no longer sleep.

Bari was sad.

At first he tried to work things out in his head.

The sea voyage was for him an unhappy memory like a dream in
which he had been compelled to fly through a stormy sky.

What a nightmare!

Well, at least he was on solid ground now.

Bari stretched out on his side.

It's not heaving up and down? No. So, I can relax and try to
understand what's going on in this house.

What's this?

Bari sniffed.

There was, predominantly, this smell of damp coal, like the smell in
the basement of the London house when he was just a puppy and still
chased rats.

Bari opened one eye.

Primo, there are no rats here. *Secundo*, a grown dog does not chase
rats.

Bari sniffed again.

That appetizing smell of food, like the smell in the butler's pantry!

Bari got up and padded over to the door of the provision store. On
the way, he caught another whiff of vetiver which tickled his nostrils.
He sneezed and swerved towards his master. But Dan Yack took no
notice of him.

Very well then, what should I do, and where am I?

Bari went back to the stove.

He pricked up his ears.

In the distance he could hear the cold walking about on the ice.

He snarled.

In the first place, why are there so many people here?

I'm not used to this, when I want to sleep. There, behind me and to my right, is the individual who stinks of poverty, like a tramp or a scoundrel.

He turned towards Goischman, sniffed him at a distance of three paces, to make sure there was no mistake, then barked at him.

The man did not budge.

Bari went back and lay down. For a long time the hair on his neck remained ruffled up. He dreamed that this man smelled of cold, of frost, night and death.

It's because of him that we're here.

Bari growled.

Usually, when he growls, someone soothes him, strokes him. He looks at his master. He no longer understands what is happening. Dan Yack does not stir (what he is doing? He's lying down, not moving, but he's not asleep). Bari goes over to Sabakov who is a friend, pure and simple.

Ivan gets up, takes his mess tin, gives the dog something to eat and strokes his neck.

That's it. That's the way things should be, thinks Bari. This man smells of fat. Paraffin, coal, burnt fat, I know that smell. He's a peasant.

He slumps down heavily on his belly.

He warms himself.

By the fire.

What a strange and disturbing thing it is!

It dazzles you.

Tongues of red meat lick you.

Bloody flesh rises, smoking, to the sky.

The sun.

A plate that is perpetually full. Although you cannot eat it, it gives off a succulent vapour that adds its own flavour to whatever falls into your jaws.

It is the sun that gives food its fragrance.

Life.

A fragrance of carrion flesh.

That is why too much sun is tiring, a kind of indigestion.

It is often as bitter as bile.

Yellow and green with flies.

Urine.

That makes him itch.

Bari scratches behind his ear, then under his foreleg, finally he gnaws at the root of his tail, which almost makes him faint.

No, it's not that.

All his senses are alert.

There are plenty of fleas burrowing into his skin, laying eggs, copulating, teeming, making him sore; but what really makes him itch is . . .

An odour of decaying flesh, a light fragrance of the sun, a scent of vanilla laced with a dash of urine, something which smells hot, and sweet, and bitter.

Bari is sitting in front of André Lamont. Fidgeting. He wags his tail. He slobbers. He is not mistaken. It is here that this smell is smeared over the floor. It is making a puddle. It is wet. It runs down this man's legs, trickles out of his trousers. It is syrupy. He would really like to lap it up. It smells of marrow, sickly and faintly putrefied marrow. How good it is!

But once more a wave of vetiver strikes his keen sense of smell. It is as violent as a crack of the whip. Bari goes back to his master. He watches him. He questions him (what is Dan Yack doing, quite motionless, as if he'd gone off on a journey?). He goes back to the fire and lies down. He dreams once more of the beeswax polish of England.

The furniture.

A splendid waxed parquet floor.

It is slippery.

He loses his footing.

He is disorientated.

Then, tired out, he dreams.

He dreams that Dan Yack is whistling for him, making him run in a howling wind, forcing him to cross crevasses, abandoning him in the snow.

No, I will not obey.

Bari has a horror of the snow.

He had never seen it until he came to Balleny and he cannot get used to it.

Why?

Yet he was a prize animal, a champion.

Bari was an English St Bernard with long curly hair, the product of selective breeding and a victim of fashion. His head was aquiline, like a sheep's, the stop was not at all pronounced, the nose pointed, the ears small and barely attached, the expression a little lack-lustre, the eyes too red. He reached ninety-five centimetres at the shoulders, which meant that his back was slightly curved and his front paws seemed rather weak and rickety. He was somewhat lacking in energy and vigour and moved softly, like all giant albinos. His coat was pure white. Dan Yack had paid a thousand guineas for him. Apparently, since 1887, English breeders have always tried to create veritable prodigies in terms of height and weight, and they achieve these results to the detriment of the animal's health. Thus, all the characteristics of the pure hospice-type St Bernard, those prime qualities of alertness and vivacity, have been sacrificed.

Bari was not playful.
But, what was more serious, he had never had a bitch.
He had tried, but in vain.
All the same, André Lamont smelled good.
He smelled like a bitch.
Bari went back to him.
Wagging his tail.
Well, what now?

Dan Yack was concerned with only three things: time, the fear of breaking his monocle, and this burdensome chastity he didn't know how to deal with.

The most pressing of the three was time; the most worrying, the fragility of his monocle; the most novel, chastity.

Since André Lamont had thrown his chronometer on the floor and stamped on it (and he had so enjoyed hearing it chime during the night), Dan Yack had been worried about the time, or rather, it was the flight of time that preoccupied him.

'What a fine thing habit is! I've always woken up at seven o'clock in the morning. So it must be seven o'clock!' he said to himself every day as he leapt out of his bunk.

And he pulled a face at André Lamont, which put him into a good humour for the rest of the day, as it gave him the feeling that he had got the better of André and he was proud of that.

'I had to take my revenge,' Dan Yack said to himself each time.

Dan Yack had plenty of other ways of counting the weeks and the months that were passing, and what a splendid, what an amusing calendar he had devised with the cans, the rows of preserves and foodstuffs!

Dan Yack put on his cap with the ear-flaps, slipped on his felt boots and an enormous pair of mittens and went into the black and icy provision store.

In there he was all alone.

What a delightful almanac!

The hurricane lamp he was holding lit up a row of twenty-four sugar-loaves whose white peaks emerged from thick blue wrapping-paper, like the unsuspected snowy peaks one discovers when exploring a new continent.

Tin cans gleamed in the shadows like seams of silver ore; there were jars of pickled cucumbers like malachite and asparagus like stalagmites. From the ceiling York hams hung like flying foxes or hibernating fruit-bats and, like absurd Coleoptera with zinc elytrona and diaphanous wings, the printed labels fluttered prettily in the beams of the lantern, whose light brought into brilliant focus a colourful pineapple or a red and orange ox-tongue. At the bottoms of the serried jars the landscapes of civilization rested serenely.

'To think that I have gathered together the world's finest produce and that those fellows in there hardly touch it,' said Dan Yack to himself. 'I had reckoned on two loaves of sugar a month and there are still four over! The same with the meat, there are far too many tins! I'm going to chuck them all out, otherwise I shall lose track of my accounts and calculations.'

Dan Yack counted and recounted his tins of meat and set them up once more in orderly stacks.

'One tin her head per day. Here we have twenty-eight for the week. And four for Bari makes thirty-two. One, two, three, four, five, six piles of thirty-two brings us up to the return of the sun. Tomorrow must be the 23rd June, the winter solstice. Add on another twice three hundred and eighty-four, let's say eight hundred for six months, that'll be more than enough to keep us going till the *Green Star* arrives.'

Dan Yack stuffed four sugar-loaves and sixty cans of meat into a sack, put on his snow-shoes and went out of the cabin, whistling for his dog.

Sometimes, with the sack on his back, he walked for long distances.

Nine times out of ten, the weather was overcast, but when it was not, the night outside was like fairyland. The icy cold was always intoxicating. And it was with a kind of exaltation that Dan Yack emptied his sack into a crevasse on the shore.

He was not stocking up a secret cache. No. He was staking his all. Risking everything. With fury and reckless joy.

'What an absurd country!' he said to himself, bursting into laughter, 'Here, summer is winter and Christmas will fall in the warmest season!'

There are six moons in the sky, a parhelion with circles, semicircles, a flickering Maltese cross and bishops' crosiers that vanish and reappear swiftly, or, sometimes, there is an austral dawn that shakes out its crackling draperies at the level of the ice; it is yellow, green, shot with fugitive gleams and punch-flames.

Dan Yack goes back at a run. 'Hey, Bari didn't come with me! What a dope!'

If Sabakov is wandering about, Dan Yack shouts a 'Good morning!' to him from a distance.

Dan Yack erupts into the house like a bomb.

The thermometer often records forty-six degrees below zero.

The meal has to be prepared. Dan Yack busies himself over the Primus. He arranges his menus according to the three-colour system of the labels, but allows himself to be seduced by the mouth-watering inscriptions which reveal the country of origin.

So many races, so many different climates, so many men have taken care of us, he thinks. I still have a hundred and sixty pots of orange marmalade. Today, I'm going to break with routine and serve them up a *buisson de guayamù.*

He goes back into the food store.

Seventeen jars of Tiflis peaches stare at him.

He fancies them.

And if I've made a mistake? he wonders with sudden anxiety. If the *Green Star* doesn't get here by Christmas? Let's say there's an extra month of pack-ice, what if the ice is denser this year? If it extends farther north than usual? If the *Green Star* can't break through it? What will become of us?

'Bah!' he says nonchalantly to himself. 'We'll die of starvation and suffer a bit, like a real polar expedition! This evening, I'll cook them a rum omelette.'

Then he takes out some orange marmalade and a large jar of peaches.

'I still have four spare packets of macaroni, I'll tip them into the snow tomorrow.'

Heads or tails?

What a gamble!

'The only thing I'm worried about is my monocle. I'm clumsy and not used to doing the cooking. It's so fragile, and with all this juggling with crates and casseroles, I could easily have an accident. Ach, what the hell, I'll make a bet on it! If I break it, we'll be buggered, and if I don't, the *Green Star* will get here on time.'

As usual the meal is gloomy. Nobody says a word. Dan Yack thinks about Billy, his manservant, who has forgotten to pack half a dozen spare monocles for him.

'I'm going to give him a rocket,' he tells himself. 'How shall I manage without a monocle?'

As soon as the meal is dispatched, the coffee drunk, a tot of anis swallowed, Dan Yack goes back into his berth and counts up.

'Six and six, twelve. Three times twelve, thirty-six. Twice thirty-six, seventy-two. We've still got seventy-two Sundays to spend on this island. No, I'm wrong, we've got only thirty-six. Thirty-six. Good. Then it will be Christmas.'

Then he caresses the big welded packing-case that contains, within a triple casing of tin, the sixty-pound plum pudding which he has had made and put on board secretly.

What a surprise! he thinks. What a splendid surprise it will be for the crew of the *Green Star*! But not for these geezers here, they really don't give a bugger. Nothing gives them any pleasure.

Dan Yack thinks about his companions. He is intrigued. What can they do?

'One claims to be a musician, but he doesn't like my gramophone records, and that hairy Goischman doesn't speak, doesn't eat, but just sits there sucking a pen-holder and pulling his nose.'

'The little Russian is nice,' says Dan Yack to himself. 'One day I must take him outside and talk to him. I wonder what he's going to do with himself? Perhaps he'll be bored stiff!'

'But what about Bari? Why is he always sitting at Lamont's feet? The traitor!'

Dan Yack becomes sorrowful.
He creeps back into the main room.
He doesn't want to disturb anyone.
He lies down on his bunk. He winds up a very small phonograph he
has brought, a pocket-sized machine, neat and reliable, which doesn't
make much noise. Dan Yack pushes the earpieces into his ears and
reels off a record that speaks to him of his chastity, sings about it,
wallows in it, rolls it about like shingle in the sea.

rerererererererererererer ererererererer ererererererrrrrrrrrrrrrrrrrrr-
rrrrrrr rrrrrrrrrrrr. *Je n'ai dansé qu'une fois avec ell-le* leurleurleur
leureureureureurerererrrrrrrrrrrrrrrrrrrrrrrrrrrrrrrrrrr. *Ce n'est pas une
femme qui est faite pour toi-oi* ouarouarouaroua roiroiroiroiroirrrer-
erererererrrrrrrrrrrrrrrrrrrrr J'ai senti son corps fou. Elle m'embrassait
dans le cou* our our our ourerererere rrrrrrrrrrrrrrrrrrrrrrrrrrrrrrrrrrr-
rrrrrrrrrrrrrrrr *Un jour pour elle ça pourrait mal tourner* erererererer-
erererrr rrrrrrrrrrrrrrrrrr rrrrrrrrrr. *Sur les bords de la Riviéra
                      Où les femmes sont toutes si joli-ies*
ieuresieuresieuresieureserererererererrrrrrrrrrrrrrrrrrrrrrrrrrrrrrrrrr
rrrrrre rrrrrrrrrrrrrrrrr

Dan Yack lies quite still. Two little white rubber plugs in his ears.
From time to time his heart swells like the heart of a drowned man
when he has just been fished out of the sea and someone is trying to
revive him by rhythmical traction on the tongue.
What a deep sigh!
Bari, who is watching his master, lies down again, disappointed.
Nothing stirs.
Nothing but the coal, shifting occasionally in the grate.
Or the accordion of the wind.
Or the ice cracking.
A heavy sigh.
'What a fine thing habit is!' says Dan Yack, suddenly jumping out
of his bunk. 'I always wake up at seven in the morning. So, it must be
seven o'clock.'
And he pulls a face at Lamont.
He is in a good mood.
But has he really slept?

PART FOUR

◆━◆━◆━◆━◆━◆━◆━◆━◆━◆━◆━◆━◆━◆━◆━◆━◆━◆━◆

THE SUN

For a week now, Dan Yack and Ivan Sabakov had been climbing Mount Brown together to watch for the reappearance of the sun. It was Dan Yack who had made the first overtures and they had held long conversations out in the open. They had discovered, to the surprise of neither, that they got on well together.

'Tell me,' Dan Yack complained, 'tell me why my dog Bari never stays with me any more. Why doesn't he want to come out, why does he stay curled up at the feet of that detestable creature? I'll kill him!'

'No, no,' interrupted Ivan Sabakov, trying to soothe him, 'don't do that. Bari is a dear old thing, I spoil him as much as I can, and he's very attached to you, you know.'

'Naturally,' Dan Yack went on. 'But tell me, why does he always sit with that sorry specimen who is also your friend. . . .'

At mention of André Lamont, a sour note was liable to creep into their conversations.

'I owe him everything,' Sabakov explained to Dan Yack, 'that is to say, he and Arkadie licked me into shape, they helped me a lot.'

'Have they lent you money? You know my wallet is always open.'

'Oh, I know that very well!' Sabakov protested warmly. 'But that's not what I meant. Without Arkadie and André,' he explained again, 'I would have spent a long time trying to find myself. They helped me to get started. But now . . .'

'Now?'

'Well, I certainly don't think as they do any more, I even despise them a little.'

'Why?'

'Because of their eccentric ideas, and because of you.'

'Because of me?'

'Yes, because of you. You've shown me how vast the world is. I never suspected it. You have opened my eyes. You know, I think about all sorts of things here. You have never laughed at me. Art is not a

62

paradox, nor is it a witticism or a more or less amusing fashion. It is not a pose. It is a profound, obscure reality, a need that must be satisfied, like hunger, like love, and yet it is very difficult to satisfy. It is a phenomenon as complex as life itself, and in order to live one must toil and love and suffer.'

'I beg your pardon,' Dan Yack interrupted, 'but I don't understand a word of what you're trying to say. 'I ask you, why does Bari love Lamont?'

'Can one ever know such things?' Sabakov replied. 'Why indeed does one love?'

A long silence.

'Do you love your friend?' asked Dan Yack.

'Yes . . . no . . . that is, since I met you . . .'

'And Goischman?'

'Arkadie is ill. I don't know what's got into him. Does one ever know, with a poet? But I assure you that André is a great artist!'

'You think so?'

'Don't you see how hard he drives himself? He doesn't sleep any more. He's working on his symphony. He had already spoken to me about it in St Petersburg. It's a prodigious work!'

'And what about you? Aren't you bored stiff here?'

'Me?' cried Ivan Sabakov. 'Not on your life! I don't have time. You'll see what I'm going to do, as soon as the sun returns. A grandiose monument. I am ready. It will be your apotheosis!'

'What do you mean?'

'Yes, I shall build a monument that will glorify you.'

'Me, but why?'

'Because.'

'I don't understand.'

'A monument crowded with men, women and children. And you, up there at the summit. You're holding the sun in your arms. You will hold it high above your head. You will light up the world!'

'Me?' said Dan Yack and burst out laughing.

'Yes, you! Oh, I've made a close study of you, you know, I've observed all your movements, all your gestures. You are handsome.'

'What?' exclaimed Dan Yack, not knowing whether to laugh or to be angry.

'Oh, nothing,' said the mortified Ivan.

Embarrassed, the two men fell silent.

From the top of Mount Brown, the naked eye can make out Buckle

Island, Borrodaille and Young Island lying like beached whales;
barely rising above the immensity of the ice-field, they form three
shadowy little nunataks.

'The sun is very late in coming,' said Dan Yack.

'It won't come today,' Sabakov asserted.

The two men made their way back.

As they walked, Dan Yack took up his theme again.

'Well then, in your opinion, why is my dog so attached to your
friend? he asked Ivan Sabakov.

Ivan replied: 'Bari is an intelligent dog. An animal is often more
sensitive than a human being. Besides, André is an artist, that is to
say, a human being who is much closer to the true nature of things
than the ordinary run of men. And don't forget that at the moment he
is working. Certainly he must be giving off a lot of vibrations. Musical
thought carries a long way, even when it is still unformulated,
embryonic. In this state, something physical must already enter into
its constitution, something analogous to and parallel with the laws of
interference which govern the speed of the propagation of light, the
vibrations of the ether and all those waves of motion and heat, of
which the most elementary is sound. A dog's hearing is very acute. It's
one of his most highly developed senses. Perhaps Bari can already
hear the music, or rather, the elementary rhythms that are
condensing around this human spirit in gestation, the phrases and
triplets which accumulate above this head in labour, the tonalities
and modalities which crowd in and jostle one another in an effort to
reach Lamont's eardrum and become rejuvenated. Certain rhythms
are very ancient. Ternaries, for instance, date back to the beginning of
the world. They are eternal. They must make the air vibrate, just as
prayers do as they pass over. I've noticed that Bari often pricks up his
ears, as if he could hear something passing that we do not perceive.
Probably he loves music.'

'My dear friend,' said Dan Yack, 'speak to me in Russian, if you
like, and I shall understand, but don't speak Chinese, I'm not clever
enough. As for music, I can guarantee that you are mistaken. Bari,
just like your dear friend the musician, has a horror of my
phonographs. It's very sad, but it's a fact that I have never been able to
play a tune for him.'

'In my home, in Russia, people are very superstitious. I have always
heard it said in my village that a dog is a mystical animal,' Ivan explained. 'They claim that God made him as a companion for man, to

bear all his earthly master's bad temper and even his blows. Whenever you stroke a dog, your nervous condition passes into him. It's like a discharge. Nowadays, sorcerers and healers still use dogs in cases of possession. And even shepherds, who never leave anything to chance, always swear by their dogs when they cast a spell on you. All our peasant women attribute great aphrodisiac virtues to certain kinds of dog-shit. Personally, I'm convinced that the dog is an intermediary creature between man and the other animals, a kind of lowly angel, just as there are higher angels who are intermediaries between man and God, the vigilant watchdogs of prayer, the hounds of paradise. And, since angels love music, dogs surely cannot despise it. It may be that our instruments, the woodwind, the strings and the percussion, are not pleasing to their ears.'

'Yes, they give them toothache,' said Dan Yack. 'All this is very amusing, Ivan, but don't talk to me in Russian, I don't understand it any more. As for me, it's not music I love, it's my phonographs. Is there one in your village?'

'The son of our parish priest brought one home from the town of Tambov. But his father took it to the monastery to be exorcized. He thought there was a devil in the machine.'

'No!'

'Yes! The monks exorcized the speaking-machine, then they buried it at the far end of the cemetery, in the corner reserved for suicides.'

'Perhaps they weren't so far wrong, you know. One day I must play you my record of a sea-lion,' Dan Yack promised. 'But tell me, my friend, would I be taken for a devil in your country?'

'Oh, you!' said Ivan, blushing.

'Yes, me, what would they make of me in your village, do you think?'

'You? I love you!' confessed Sabakov.

One day the shadows of the earth, projected on to the sky by the sun as it gradually sank below the northern horizon, were quite clearly visible from the summit of Mount Brown. A sombre ray, inclined to the left and forming an acute angle with the horizon, appeared very high up to the west of Young Island, with Mount Freeman to the right, partly veiled by purple clouds. Little by little, this ray moved up into a vertical position, then slanted and fell, forming an ever-diminishing angle. At the same time two other shadows were visible, one vertical, the other inclined towards the east. This phenomenon looked, therefore, like an inverted arrow.

'It's extraordinary!' cried Ivan Sabakov. 'It's as if the celestial engineer were giving an illustrated lecture, walking along behind paper models of the planets, with a candle in his hand, to demonstrate the theory of the movement of the heavenly bodies. It's splendid!'

'I think Strown Island must be somewhere in those dense lines of shadow,' said Dan Yack. 'It must be facing us, between us and the sun. It's too low to be visible from here. The seal-hunters used to call it Black Island.'

'And to think we have seen nothing but moving shadows, yet that is the sun!' cried Ivan.

'You will see the sun tomorrow,' said Dan Yack.

'Tomorrow, are you sure?'

'Yes, it's . . .'

'Promise me?'

'Yes. Besides, spring is coming.'

'How can you tell?'

'My supply of vetiver is exhausted.'

'Thank God!' shouted Ivan Sabakov. 'Dan Yack, let me embrace you! The sun! The sun! I shall be able to work!'

After a prolonged bear-hug the two men ran back to the cabin.

The sun! The sun!

Next morning Dan Yack leapt briskly out of bed.

It's after seven, he thought. I must have slept a long time, it's late!

Annoyed, he looked about him.

Bari was stretched out on Lamont's bunk. André was at his table, writing. Goischman, enormous and puffed up like a feather bed, was in his own corner. Ivan had already gone out, carrying his sculptor's tools with him.

The sun! The sun!

Wait a bit, thought Dan Yack, I have a surprise in store for you.

And he hurried about his business.

He wound up all his phonographs and all his gramophones and set them up on the big table in order of size. He put a record or a cylinder on each one. Then, moving as quickly as possible from one to the other, he set them all going. They were triggered off almost simultaneously. The turntables started to spin. There was a multiple whirring noise, then a nasal voice roared: ' "The Marseillaise"! . . . played by the trumpeters of the Garde Républicaine!'

But before the phrase was finished, overlapping with it, two other machines struck up, a quarter of a turn later, like cannons firing a salute on a day of national celebration: *Bojé Tzara chrani*. Then the Garde Républicaine broke into 'The Marseillaise' with a great fanfare of bugles and drums, while another machine burst forth with 'God Save the King' played on the bagpipes!

There was a racket fit to wake the dead. The gramophones tried to drown each other out.

'The sun! The sun!' yelled Dan Yack.

He was beaming.

He started up the last phonograph and the languorous voice of Fragson joined in the tumult: *'Manon . . . voici le . . . sssolei!'*

Bari had jumped off the bunk. André Lamont had risen to his feet as if he, too, were wound up by a spring. He held his head in both hands. He was prancing with rage.

'Ach, the bastard! The bastard!'

Goischman never flinched.

'C'est l'amour-maître des cho - o - ses,' Fragson bawled in his husky voice. The machines outdid one another in volume and tempo; they played over and over again, from the beginning; they had not yet lost their voices, unlike Dan Yack who, nevertheless, still found sufficient breath to shout 'The sun! The sun!'

Bari was barking.

Still Goischman did not budge.

'Shut up! Shut up!' Lamont shouted at Dan Yack.

The gramophones started up again, louder than ever. The room echoed to the cries of the crowd, applause, thousands of voices, trumpets, the brouhaha of processions, a million shuffling feet.

At last the Tsar died on a final, dying fall of *phew-phew*; then it was the King's turn to fall silent; 'The Marseillaise' still rolled on, warlike and democratic; it stopped abruptly on a crash of the big bass drum.

rrrrrererererearararararararararara . . . gasped the records in their death-throes.

Only the ever more languorous voice of Fragson lingered on:

Laisse-moi dans tes bras blancs
Bercer des rêves troublants
Et mon dé-sir qui se pâ-â-â-me.[5]

'What's the matter with you, are you crazy?' Lamont now yelled.

He was mad with rage. His hands flew about his body in a wild desire to strangle, to rend, to destroy. Bari was at his heels. He advanced menacingly on Dan Yack.

'Bastard, skunk, son-of-a-bitch!' he castigated Dan Yack, bumping against the table and knocking a record on to the floor, where it broke. 'But what the hell's the matter with you, have you gone mad?'

'The sun! The sun!' replied Dan Yack breathlessly.

'What sun?'

André Lamont passed his hand over his forehead. His face was ravaged. His eyes bleary. His hand blue. He seemed to have grown taller and was as desiccated as a pressed leaf dried out between sheets of blotting-paper in a dark cupboard. There was nothing left of him but skin and bone. His ears were sticking out, tufted with hair. It was the effect of the long polar night.

'What sun?' he repeated wildly.

He was tottering.

Shocked, Dan Yack drew up an armchair for him.

André slumped into it.

Huge beads of sweat ran down his face and he was trembling.

'I don't understand, what is it you're saying?' he asked again. 'What sun?'

'But . . . but . . . the sun,' stammered Dan Yack. 'The great outdoor sun. Today is the 31st of August.'

'And I thought I had destroyed it,' said André Lamont, overcome with emotion. And he started to whimper: 'Now I shall have to start all over again . . . everything. My symphony is ruined. . . . Ah, Lulu, Lulu!' he wailed.

He started sobbing.

A long silence.

Dan Yack watched him. André Lamont was lolling in the armchair, his head thrown back, his long legs stretched out and his hands dangling. He looked like a dead man, with his skinny neck, his

5   Let me in your arms so white
                     Cradle my disturbing dreams
                     And my desire, swooning with delight.

shrivelled tendons and, just as with a corpse, his hair, his eyebrows, the tufts of hair sprouting from his ears, even his nails, seemed to have grown. He was a terrifying sight. Dan Yack was struck by the subtle odour of putrefaction that emanated from this laid-out body.

'What's the matter with you?' he asked. 'Are you ill?'

'Yes,' replied André Lamont.

Dan Yack went and fetched the medicine chest.

'Are you in pain?' he asked him. 'Wait a minute, I've got everything we need here to give you some relief. Tell me what's wrong with you.'

André Lamont burst out laughing.

'You imbecile!' he replied. 'I've got syphilis.'

And he laughed again.

Then he was shaken by a fit of coughing.

And he fell silent.

'Syphilis?' said Dan Yack, alarmed.

André Lamont did not answer.

What can I do for him? Dan Yack wondered as he rummaged through the medicine chest.

Suddenly, he called Bari: 'Bari, come here!'

Bari did not move.

As a matter of fact, thought Dan Yack, ashamed, he doesn't smell good, that's why Bari never leaves his side. I'll kill him, the filthy beast!

He read a label: calomel. And he wondered if calomel was any good for syphilis.

Hey, I've got some ampoules to counteract scurvy, too. Suppose I gave him a shot?

'Would you like me to give you an injection?' he asked aloud.

'No use,' said André Lamont, 'my brain is already turning to rubber.'

He was thinking: I'm done for, I've been dragging this around with me for years.

And, aloud, he asked: 'Sorry, what did you say?'

Dan Yack was thinking: Poor devil, he was ill, and there was I making faces at him every morning!

Aloud, he said: 'Come with me. Let's go and watch the sunrise.'

Lamont did not answer.

The two men had nothing more to say to each other.

Dan Yack did not go out.

On the floor lay the fragments of the broken record. Dan Yack pushed them gently with his foot.

A profound unease held the room in thrall.

The lamps began to dim, for the first time in many long months. At last the long-awaited dawn was filling the one and only window.

A few seconds later a ray of sunlight struck Dan Yack's head, and his monocle began to blaze.

It was as swift as it was brief. And not one of the three men gathered together in the room perceived it, for, behind the monocle, Dan Yack's eye was shut. He was thinking bitterly: Bari chose between us, and attached himself to disease. Pfaugh!

Still Lamont lay there like a dead man and Arkadie Goischman was contemplating the shadow of his nose on the partition screen.

Bari was the only one who noticed this luminous bee that flew away as rapidly as it had entered.

Already dusk was drawing a curtain over the window and, outside, total darkness had descended once more.

The light of the lamps intensified a little.

A profound unease held the room in thrall. Not even the ticking of a clock was to be heard.

André Lamont and Dan Yack, in truth, no longer had anything to say to each other. As for Arkadie Goischman, he was squinting down at his nose.

'The sun! The sun!' cried Ivan Sabakov, rushing into the room like a madman. 'Danny, did you see it?'

This voice struck Dan Yack to the heart. He jumped to his feet. He wanted to say something. He dropped his monocle and it sparkled on the floor like a huge tear.

Dan Yack sat down again.

His head was spinning.

He could not say a word.

From that day on, life was never again to follow its accustomed routine in the little house under the cliff.

And there were still three months to go till Christmas!

Dan Yack was beginning to get impatient.

All the more so since his monocle was broken and he had completely lost track of his calculations of the days and weeks gone by or still to come.

Lamont, leaving his symphony unfinished, had renounced work in favour of the bottle, and now, every time Dan Yack went into the store-room after André had been there, he found the place in disorder, piles of cans knocked down, jars opened, crates broken into, casks staved in, sacks split and the month's stock or the daily rations scattered about.

This disorder upset him.

'We'll never survive till Christmas,' murmured Dan Yack, stacking up the cans again and carefully resealing the jars. One, two, three, four, five, six, seven . . . no, we'll never be able to hold out. So much the worse, God help us! Well, we shall see. But this fellow is very provocative, he's always wrecking my plans.'

And Dan Yack went out again, very woebegone.

He no longer had any point of reference.

There's a jinx on us, he thought, for, since breaking his monocle, he had lost faith in everything.

But, on the threshold, he turned half-about and went back into the provision store.

'It's still there, and he'll never find it!'

He rejoiced as he shifted the sacks beneath which he had buried the famous crate containing the sixty-pound plum pudding that, he had promised himself, was going to give so much joy at Christmas time. 'What a surprise I'll give them, if they get here!'

And he started to hope again, although he had given up counting the days.

He was free.

At last!

A man who no longer had a care in the world.

'That's the way I am.

'So be it.

'Everything makes me laugh.'

The days had been lengthening visibly and now the sun no longer set.

Ivan Sabakov, who had deserted the cabin under the cliff and elected to live under canvas in the fissure of a rock, no longer concerned himself in any way with his comrades.

He didn't have the time.

He was working flat out.

As far as the eye could see, there was nothing but an icy shroud, white ruins, *tabula rasa*.

He hadn't a minute to lose.

He was going to populate this wilderness.

Out to sea, the chaotic pack-ice was made up of a barrier of icebergs and banked-up floes which contained the debris or the sketch-plans of all the cities in the world. There was a crazy jumble of bell-towers, ramparts, feudal hamlets, Byzantine churches, Etruscan palaces, Roman circuses, Chinese pagodas, Assyrian friezes and cornices, as well as Louis-Philippe streets, obelisks and colonnades. And all this built of pure ice, an uninhabitable wasteland. An arena. A cemetery. A work-site.

The sky above, almost always overcast with cloud or daubed with mist, was often streaked with the most riotous colours or blotched with red ink, like blotting-paper.

The sun was now round, now oval; red, orange or even violet, but always lowering, very low. As it never dipped below the horizon, its lower edge was worn into a saw-toothed blade and, eventually, it flattened out like a punctured tyre. Its rays were almost horizontal, lighting objects from below, artificially exaggerating planes and volumes, unwinding shadows to immoderate lengths and giving to everything they lit upon an appearance of unreality that, day after day, left Ivan dumbfounded.

Nature flayed bare, crystallized, everything reduced to abstract geometry, the most beautiful image, the senses, the instincts, everything was intelligible, nothing obscured the luminous vision of the true nature of things; it was great art in which life was not absent but latent!

Oh, my God, what a lesson!

Ivan wandered amongst the uneven sastrugi of an immense ice-field that stretched in front of the island. He was armed with his mallet and chisel. He was making for the small ice-blocks that stood upright on this bay-ice like columellae. He moved from one block to another and, as he moved on, he left behind him a bust, a stele, a cippus, a monument, a monolithic statue, a humanized milestone or an anthropomorphic pillar of ice.

He worked swiftly, for Ivan had acquired a wonderful dexterity.

Such dexterity, and such a beautiful medium to work in! The ice was fragile, pure, luminous, transparent, faintly opaque!

Ivan Sabakov was happy.

Every one of his figures was created in the image of Dan Yack. His love.

Ivan had abandoned his idea of a grandiose and chimeric monument – 'too fussy', he said to himself now. He was working towards a synthesis. Voluptuously, he rounded the shaft of a column. On the top of it he delicately balanced an egg-shaped ball, with its point at the bottom. Then two-thirds of the way up this ball, he stuck in a disc of polished ice.

'The eye!' he said to himself.

'No, the monocle,' he at once corrected himself, aloud.

He arranged it so as to catch the sun.

He stepped back a pace to admire it.

It is not the eye that I must sculpt, but the look, the look of eternity.

The material is pure, he thought again. My forms are pure. My work is pure.

The cold was so intense that his tools burned his hands. His fingers were chapped, cracked, raw, but Ivan continued to work.

His soul was consumed by a mystical ardour. A need for purity. For intimate connection.

'I must cling even more closely to reality, to the reality that is God.'

'A circle, a square, a cube, a sphere, a disc, an ellipse are manifestations of His perfection.'

He was talking to himself.

Aloud: 'Glory be to God! I have rediscovered the Tradition. I have rediscovered the way of my father: the Truth. I no longer have the right to stop. Soon I shall have to start all over again. The summer, or the next storm, will raze my work to the ground. That's it, I've no right to stop work. Perpetual motion is the divine essence, it is the only truly creative work. It proceeds by elimination. Tirelessly. Error, for the artist, is the desire to rest on the seventh day and to rely on imperishable materials. One should cleave only unto the Spirit and the Spirit bloweth where it listeth.'

So great was Ivan Sabakov's desire for simplification and for purification that he dreamed of an incorporeal sculpture.

Ah! To burn oneself up as one brought forms into being, to create, like the sun, by radiation!

No longer to sculpt the hand, but the infinite space that circulates between the splayed fingers.

All the movements of the stars and planets.

One should no longer make an effigy, he thought, but the Being himself, or, better still, the Essence of that Being.

And now, out of the walls of icebergs, he carved nothing but immense discs of ice, which he polished until they flashed and glistened in the sun.

'Dan Yack was absolutely right to wear a monocle,' he said to himself. 'The monocle is everything.'

Man.

A crystallization.

A gel.

A micella.

God.

It began to snow lightly and Ivan caught each flake that fell into his hands and carried it to his lips.

God! God! he murmured. Thy Cross! Thy Star! Thy Ramifications! Thy Veins! Thine Eyelashes! Thine Host!

And, weeping with emotion, he took refuge in the tent.

But when the snow turned to rain, the rain condensed into thick mists and the weather closed in in earnest, and the storm burst through the sudden darkness with a furious clashing of nearby cymbals and a distant tumult of drums, Ivan Sabakov hastily put on his skis and made his way back to the cabin under the cliff. Blinded and dazzled, Sabakov did not battle against the unleashed elements. The hurricane was so saturated with electricity that the fire of St Elmo flashed from the points of his skis and surrounded the whole of Ivan's person with a pale aureole of crackling plumes. He let himself be swept along by the wind. He pivoted, he spun round in the eddies, but a very sure instinct, which he took to be divine Providence, brought him back each time in the direction of the cabin. Once there, he flopped on to his bunk and immediately fell into the sleep of the blessed.

His dreams were rimed with ice. But, at the first break in the weather, he went out again to work. He took off like an arrow into the virginal morning. The air was rarefied, it smelled of ozone. The sun was a little higher than usual. Ivan set out on the ascending path. He was going to capture it at last. He was sure of it. He was filled with the bold self-confidence of one who is young and pure and has just taken communion!

Ivan no longer took the slightest interest in his companions and, without its monocle, the face of Dan Yack struck him as diabolical.

'Brrr!' he said as he polished a freshly cut disc of ice which scintillated in the sun, reflecting its rays and throwing off flames.

'The only possible sculpture is light.

'I shall achieve my aim.

'Like an angel.'

And, setting the wheel of ice he had just fashioned on its rim, he sent it rolling down to the bottom of a slope.

'Adieu! Yack!' he shouted. 'My love!'

Hurtling down at ever-increasing speed, the ice-wheel threw off sparks before it shattered and flew into a thousand fragments.

In spite of the terrible south-east wind that had relentlessly brought down the temperature and provoked hurricanes of appalling violence, it was after all summer. Spells of fine weather, lasting for several days, were fairly frequent.

Then Dan Yack would open the window.

And through the open window they could hear the intermittent cannonade of the pack-ice out at sea and the much closer thunder of the immense tabular icebergs that came aground on the very shores of the islet. This crescendoing racket, more intense every day, heralded the coming thaw and was yet another grandiose and precursory sign of summer.

However, it was not these sounds, or the sporadic fusillade, or the resounding explosions provoked by the first swell of the ocean, which drew Arkadie Goischman out of his torpor. In the silence of this long winter's night he had lain doggo in his corner, like a hibernating bear or a marmot, taking refuge in the deepest part of his being so as to nourish himself on his own substance, eating his heart out, and the volley of invective, insult, sarcasm, curses and blasphemies that he addressed to himself had, in quite another manner, battered at his poor head and unhinged his reason.

Arkadie Goischman held his nose in his hand, and he held it tight, and he clung to it, against the evanescence of a multitude of scruples, ceaselessly reborn, that passed through his mind as he pondered on his impotence and was driven to despair of his very life.

What injustice! He could not even account for himself.

He felt that he was dying.

He was numb.

He was always cold.

Freezing to the marrow.

Misery!

Now, what was drawing him little by little out of this nightmare was the sun, which fell directly on to his bed whenever Dan Yack opened the window.

The sun fell on him, wrapped him, as it were, in a soft quilted cover, then it bound him up and breathed its scorching breath down his back. And soon the sunlight became cruel, it spread throughout the length of his exhausted body, dug its fiery claws into his temples and stared at him, eyeball to eyeball. An intolerable burning penetrated his closed eyelids, the veins of his eyes glowed like white-hot needles, and when Arkadie Goischman tried to open his mouth, his cry of pain died in his throat, suffocated by a brazier that shrivelled his lungs, took away his breath and stopped his heart as effectively as the thrust of a spear or a draught of molten glass.

When at last he opened his eyes, it was only to contemplate his nose.

He squinted.

It was horrible.

Oh, God, to return to life in such a pitiful condition!

What misery! He felt he was dying.

He was freezing.

Slowly.

To the marrow.

The sun was reviving him, but for what? Nothing but an atrocious, an intolerable burning.

One day his physical sufferings forced him to sit up on his bunk. The window was open. The room was full of sunlight. Arkadie Goischman who, by a considerable effort of will had succeeded in dragging his eyes away from the hooked bridge of his nose, looked to right and left about the room. His eyes, his poor, bloodshot eyes, staggered about, bumping into objects like a blind man. Through a kind of red mist they recognized two vague human forms, Dan Yack, with his back turned, surrounded by a triple halo as he stood against the light from the window, and André Lamont, dazzling, faceted, even more iridescent than the carafe of kümmel he was in the process of opening.

Arkadie Goischman tried to stand up. He couldn't move his legs. They were swollen, enormous, inert, stabbed by a million pins and needles, gnawed by itching and no longer obedient to his will; they were as if detached from his body, alien, two mortadella sausages peppered with scurf, turning blue, livid, numb, trussed up and ravaged by oedema. The effort of throwing off his blankets had exhausted him. His heart was pounding like a steam-hammer, then it stopped dead and it was a moment before it started beating again, irregular, tachycardic, painful.

Goischman went mad with fright. It was crazy. He could feel the cold invading his body, paralysing his back and kidneys. And yet there was all this sunshine in the room, which should have . . .

Stark terror!

'Men attacked by scurvy are deprived of the conversation of others and reduced to a solitary life,' he had read some time ago in a very old work by Corneille Falconnet, a physician from Lyons. The phrase had imprinted itself on his mind as if on a screen. He remembered the large, bold typography of the old tome, and a faint odour of mildew and damp-stains wafted into his brain.

'André, I'm dying!' he cried with all his strength.

He had scarcely whispered, and three teeth fell out of his mouth.

He slipped off his bunk.

André Lamont had heard nothing, but Dan Yack, who was looking through his telescope at the transverse crevasses appearing in the surface of the ice, turned round, having heard a sort of rattle and a dull thud on the floor.

Goischman was lying on his stomach.

'Ah, it's you,' he groaned when Dan Yack leaned over him and put his arms around him. 'Help me stand up, I can't move any more. I'm cold.'

Dan Yack carried him over to an armchair and pushed the chair up to the stove. He poked the fire, which had burned low, as often happened now that Ivan was no longer there to tend it.

Bari ran round the two men, barking.

'Lie down!' Dan Yack shouted at him.

And, as the dog failed to obey, he attacked André Lamont: 'Hey, you, can't you keep your bloody dog quiet?'

André lifted his head and smiled, but did nothing. Then Dan Yack snatched his knife, aimed it downward and threw it at the dog. The blade missed Bari by a hair's breadth and stuck into the floor-boards, between Goischman's swollen feet. Arkadie looked at it, quivering in the sunlight.

'It's nothing,' said Dan Yack. 'Keep calm, I'll make you some grog.'

He busied himself, lit the Primus, went out to get a panful of snow, came back, set it over the paraffin flame and disappeared once more into the provision store.

'We've already finished the lemons,' he murmured, 'and soon there'll be no rum left. Too bad!'

He drew off a quarter-litre of rum and went back to Goischman's side.

Goischman was alone in the big room. The door was open. Lamont had gone. And Bari was not there either.

Dan Yack threw down the rum and rushed outside.

Lamont had already reached the foot of the cliff. Dan Yack saw him climbing over the little icicle-festooned seracs on the shore so as to reach the ice-field beyond. It was the first time he had ventured out there and the slightest obstacle in his path seemed too much for him. Bari had already gone on ahead. Dan Yack noticed that Lamont was bareheaded and that he was holding a bottle in his hand.

'André!' he shouted, cupping his hands into a megaphone. 'André! Come back! Put on your cap and goggles or you'll go snowblind!'

Lamont did not answer. Perhaps he did not even hear, for, at that very moment, he fell and skidded along on his bottom.

'Look out!' shouted Dan Yack again. 'Don't go out on the ice-field, it's full of crevasses!'

But Lamont, who had scrambled to his feet again, crossed the moraine and set out resolutely on to the bay-ice. He was following Bari, who was well ahead but stopped every ten paces to let him catch up.

Dan Yack watched as he moved farther out, floundering painfully in the spongy ice, clumsily leaping across fissures, zigzagging, working his way round icebergs, disappearing behind hummocks, being swallowed up in the long white foothills of the ice. Staggering more and more wildly. A little black dot. A fly. Then Dan Yack lost sight of him.

He's drunk, he thought. But why did he go out today? I must go and warn Ivan. He's bound to have an accident.

Anxiously, he inspected the sky.

The horizon to the north was a long black line.

'Water! Open water! Open water!' he shouted, 'There's open water!'

He was beside himself with joy.

Open water!

From where he stood, he could not see the sea. The pack-ice stretched to the far horizon, motionless. But just above this extreme limit, he could see a black margin bordering the sky. There could be no mistake, it was undoubtedly the far-off reflection of the waters. The ocean!

The sea must have melted during the morning, thought Dan Yack, I may be able to see it from the top of Mount Brown.

And he started climbing the peak.

He was wildly excited.

I must tell Ivan the good news. How happy that boy will be!

Dan Yack climbed up slowly, moving one foot at a time. He clung to the rock like a limpet. It was friable and slippery. In places, the snow was melting and the reverberations as it fell were deafening. The slope was exposed to the sun and, for the first time, cascades of water were gurgling down its sides. To avoid them, Dan Yack straddled a perpendicular ridge and hauled himself up, fist over fist. He looked upward, fearing an avalanche. He still had to scale a chimney, covered in scree that was now loose and crumbling, then a col and finally the summit.

Suddenly he thought of Goischman.

I've abandoned him!

He was hanging in the void, without crampons, quite near the summit, with his nose against the warm stone.

I didn't give him his hot grog!

And he let himself slither down the scree. It was a vertiginous slide and rapidly brought him down to the level of the house.

Before going in, he cast a final look at the sky. The southern horizon, pristine, diamantine, held his attention. A sea-mist, a tenuous, almost imperceptible vapour was condensing at the zenith and whirling round, very high up in the air. There was no wind. Yet this sea-mist could be seen rapidly encroaching, growing thicker in sudden puffs and blotting out a quarter of the horizon. It was as if a cloud of very fine dust had been thrown into the sky, tarnishing its brilliance, dulling the sun and turning the long shadows of the icebergs green.

'It's a blizzard. It'll be here within an hour. The great thaw will come tonight,' said Dan Yack to himself as he went into the house.

At his back, the first shrill whistles of the wind, then a dull thud, like a detonation. It was the pack-ice moving.

Goischman was still in front of the fire. Dan Yack couldn't make him out very clearly, for the room was full of smoke; the water on the Primus had boiled dry and the Nansen cooker was red-hot.

A noxious smell of melting tin, asphyxiating gas and paraffin caught him by the throat.

Dan Yack coughed, his eyes were smarting. He called out: 'Goischman, are you asleep?'

'Ah! Is that you?' Goischman replied. 'I was waiting for you. Come, come here, I've got a present for you. Take it, here's my nose.'

And he held out some filthy object wrapped in a blood-soaked rag.

Only then did Dan Yack notice the knife Goischman was holding in his hand, and his face, split open like a burst drum, with a hole in the middle.

'I've cut off my nose, I've cut off my nose, like Van Gogh,' explained Arkadie Goischman. 'I give it to you, oh, my ——.'

Dan Yack had fled.

He ran.

The first squalls of the storm dragged at his legs.

He ran with every ounce of his strength.

'Ivan, Ivan,' he was murmuring, 'look what they're trying to do to me!'

He stopped at the end of the promontory.

So strong were the gusts of wind that already he had to battle against them to keep on his feet. An immense frieze of clouds hung from the sky and shook like a vast canopy. Through its rents and tears, its fitful openings, the sun exploded in a spatter of colour that was like the beams of a thousand magic lanterns, whirling, criss-crossing, focusing at this point. Above this maelstrom of vivid splotches that spun deliriously, ecstatically, like crazy tops, the diapason of the wind grew louder by the second. Now it slid right across the ice-field in one continuous stroke like the movement of a razor, and in its wake there opened long fissures, zigzagging rifts, a network of fine cracks and gashes like wounds, from between those gaping lips spurted a black and seething water. Jets of foam spouted up. Enormous icebergs turned somersaults. Ice-floes mounted on top of one another, grappled and crushed each other furiously. Rammed by the motion of the sea, the pack-ice was hurled into the air and the floes fell back, roaring like heavy shells and sending up waterspouts. Everything was in collision, breaking up, shattering into smithereens, dislocated and, seized with frenzy, flung itself hysterically into the fray. Everything was breaking loose, emptying itself out from above or below, everything was cutting adrift, tumultuous, bewildered, in total disarray, faltering, sucked in, spat out in the hurly-burly of flight, the thronging, the panic of the elements in chaos, of nature put to rout by the stinging, cracking lash of the blizzard.

In this universal débâcle Dan Yack searched only for Ivan. He wanted to reach him, to reach him at all costs, stand beside him, shake his hand. There were so many things he had to say to him, so many things to apologize for. He didn't give a damn about the thaw, the open water, the imminent arrival of the ship. He wanted to justify himself, to explain himself, to make Ivan understand that . . .

He searched everywhere for him, in his tent, in a fault in the rock, on an ice-floe that was floating away, in the air, on the land, out at sea; in the depths of his own heart.

'Ivan, Ivan,' he murmured.

And from time to time he stopped and cried out with all his might: 'Ivan! Ivan!'

The hurricane forced him to his knees, so he dragged himself along on all fours. He searched. He crawled along flat on his stomach. He leapt over a crevasse. By prodigious feats of energy and daring he succeeded in crossing the channels full of eddying currents to reach the submerged ice-floes that were being carried away in the flood. Ice-needles pricked his eyes like splinters of glass, the spindrift froze him, weighed him down, the wind lassoed him, time and again, binding him ever more painfully, tightening the knots till they cut into his flesh, strangling him. Dan Yack kept going. He searched. Ceaselessly.

He had to find Ivan, he had to unburden his heart to him, it was a matter of life or death! He wanted to justify himself, explain, make him understand that . . .

'Go on, keep marching. Onward. You'll find him. He will understand, he will . . . Ivan!'

The sky had turned livid, the light had faded to dusk. The pack-ice gave off fiery reflections. Dan Yack, perched on a rickety hummock of ice, scanned the distance. He thought he could make out a dim black figure. Something stretched out, several miles away. Something blurred in the distance. He took his bearings. There were two long arms of the sea to cross, then a battlefield where the bombardment of ice-floes, the explosion of icebergs and submarine mines, the destruction, the massacre was particularly intense. Cataclysm. Earthquake. The eye of the hurricane.

The sea, the wind, the unleashed clouds and the slingshot of the ice.

Dan Yack overcame all these obstacles.

It took him hours and hours, perhaps a whole day.

But he succeeded.

When he got there, he found himself on a fragile ice-floe that was bobbing up and down in the deluge like a cork.

In vain Dan Yack called Ivan.

What, from the distance, he had taken to be a human being stretched out was, in reality, a block of black ice, that earthy ice which glaciologists call 'fossil ice'.

But what a strange shape this block was. One would have thought it was a statue toppled by the storm.

The black block had arms, legs, a torso. It had fallen on to its stomach. The head had been knocked off.

Dan Yack picked up this head. It was his own. His nose. His forehead. His chin. His mouth.

A striking resemblance.

There was no monocle in the eye and the eye was smiling.

Punctiliously.

Dan Yack was thunderstruck. Then he searched further and took a closer look. He picked up a wooden mallet, then a chisel. A long file. Finally, beneath the belly of the monstrous statue, he discovered Ivan Sabakov, crushed to death.

Ivan was tiny.

Ivan was no longer alive.

What irony! A question of life or death? Dan Yack no longer had anything to say to him.

Every man for himself.

The hurricane has been raging for days now.

The wind has just shifted. It is blowing a mixture of snow and verglas.

A small lake, formed by the melting of the ice during the first few days of summer, has just emptied itself like an overturned cup.

A swollen, crepuscular light.

It is raining.

Everything is dancing in a runnel of water.

Everything is shaking itself out, winding itself up again.

It is snowing.

A lull.

New ice has blossomed like flowers and young shoots, the shores are pearly, as if painted in water-colours, the beaches are too fragile to venture upon.

A mirage.

Translucent ice-floes.

The sun is bleary-eyed.

It rains, it snows, it blows. The wind shifts again. The hurricane returns with renewed force.

Everything is drowned in salty tears.

Everything howls.

The sea pounds furiously.

It is freezing hard enough to crack stones.

The hurricane holds sway.

It is freezing.

Never before has Arkadie Goischman been so lucid.

The fire has died out long ago and a destructive giant is wrecking everything in the house.

The hurricane has come in through the open door, and immediately knocked down the lamps. It has smashed in the window. It is breaking and plundering everything. Pressing its back to the wall, it flexes its muscles, rages, tramples, howls and bursts into a nerve-racking laugh. There's a sound of crockery breaking, doors slamming. A thousand whistles, a thousand roars. Furniture is blown about the room, revolving. Floor-boards are wrenched up. A sheet of iron flies off the roof in terror. Books flap their wings.

The house is filled with wind.

It sighs, surrenders.

First the roof flies off, then the back wall collapses. Then to right and left the partition walls are blown away, they disappear, once and for all. The only thing left standing is the absurd, shattered pane of the window and, in front of this window, Arkadie Goischman in his armchair. The wind spins him round but always brings him back, face to face with this useless window. He is covered in rime and snow.

Arkadie Goischman remains impassive.

He sees the Primus overturn and the paraffin flames run towards him, licking his legs and his chair.

Never has Arkadie been so lucid.

He puts his hand to his nose.

He thinks proudly: The death of a man of letters. I am dying of a plagiarism, and even this plagiarism is botched.

In fact, Van Gogh only cut off his right ear, and, moreover, it was for a woman. Whereas I! . . .

He despises himself, with pride.

Futility.

Mental lucidity.

He burns.

He freezes.

He blazes.

An iceberg turns upside-down and disintegrates. In its fall, it brings down rags of tattered mist.

A dome of blue sky, then a luminous rift that descends right down to the level of the seething water.

A ray of sunlight is sprinkled over the mountains of floating ice, which break up and distil its light.

Everywhere, dazzling light. The rainbow is knotted into a whirlwind of sapphires, emeralds, rubies; it is a constantly shaken kaleidoscope, changing, splintering, reflecting and refracting.

André Lamont, prostrate on an ice-floe, is carried out to sea.

He is lost.

Bari jumps into the water and swims desperately amongst the eddying currents.

He wants to go back.

He barks. And barks.

He struggles.

The pack-ice answers him with lugubrious roars, bleatings, a human voice, the canticle of the angels, the sighs of demons.

Bari pricks up his ears and sinks like a stone.

The mist is viscous.

The sea breaks up.

It is choppy.

Everything is rocking.

Dan Yack is demoralized.

The ice-floe he is on carries him to and fro, spinning round on itself, the plaything of all the dallying currents, the victim of collisions that break off or erode its edges and cause it to melt.

Once again the ice-floe receives a violent impact. It recoils. And then a final shock from below lifts it up and splits it in two. And while Dan Yack, clinging to the broken-off stump, is whirled away in an eddy, he sees the other half capsize, the block of fossil-ice rear up, the black statue take a few steps in the air before the whole thing, with its prey, the inert body of Ivan Sabakov, still clamped to it, is swept away, bobbing wildly, and smashes to pieces against a projecting outcrop of rock. It bursts with the violence of an explosion. The belly of the monstrous statue is pulverized. A hail of ice-splinters (they are round and polished, like monocles) flies in all directions and Ivan's corpse describes a wide trajectory before falling to earth again in the distance. The wind shifts yet again and it begins to snow.

A profound calm.

It is still snowing.

Dan Yack shakes off the white shroud that covers him.

He has been washed ashore at the end of the promontory. Painfully, he climbs the steep path that leads to the house. When he gets there, he finds not a trace of the house. The blackened timbers rise out of a heap of debris buried under the snow.

It is still snowing.

Everything is white.

The wind has dropped at last.

How silent it is!

Dan Yack does not search for anything.

He does not want anything.

He simply collects a few scattered planks, arranges them in the form of a cross and nails them together. Then he plants this cross in the middle of the charred ruins.

Since this cross is made from odds and ends of boards, and these boards have come from old disused packing-cases, one can read, on the front or back, across the top or bottom, the words PICON, VERMOUTH, and the trade mark of BLACK BULL whisky, as well as the name of a famous champagne.

It is the longest day of the year.

PART FIVE

PORT DECEPTION

The island was completely deserted; Dan Yack had explored all over it several times.

Nothing ever happened.

There was nothing but the vast unfolding of nature, with its storms, its blustery winds and, in calm weather, the palpable ebb and flow that washed the floating ice, the flotilla of ice-floes, the squadron of icebergs away from the shore and back in again. Everything moved to and fro in perpetual motion: the great continental clouds, like a ship's crew in seamen's jerseys, worked their way across a sky that was concave, a deserted sports drome; the humped backs of the hollowed-out waves; the punctual sun that turned and turned, silent as a gramophone record on which nothing had been recorded, dumb as a virgin disc.

There were no animals on the island. Only a little snow petrel that flew over at regular intervals, quite low, gliding round in a circle, describing figures of eight, while its head and its lidless eye swivelled in all directions, before it flew out to sea again with long, melancholy strokes of the wing, strong, rhythmical strokes, returning whence it came without so much as a cry.

One day this petrel shed a downy feather and Dan Yack watched it for a long time, this frail white feather, too light to come down to earth.

And that was a significant event.

Dan Yack had yet another distraction which occurred once a day, towards evening. This was the arrival of an old elephant seal, a solitary old female that splashed about in the shallows below the promontory; from time to time she would lift her head out of the water, look at Dan Yack and snort.

He contemplated her from the shore without moving.

Did she amuse him? Did he amuse her? Yes and no. Yes and no. He himself did not know. At any rate he was not bored.

He had not a care in the world. Not one. The only thing that sometimes weighed on him was his chastity. It was becoming more and more burdensome, oppressive and, in spite of himself and of his efforts to fight against it, on certain days he found himself thinking of Hedwiga. From the moment he woke up.

Hedwiga . . .

And not a single gramophone to distract him from thinking about her.

Hedwiga . . .

Happily, there was always his beard to annoy and distract him, this beard that was growing on his chin and which he did not know how to get rid of, since he no longer had a razor, this beard which was like a noxious weed, the only vegetation on the island.

Apart from that, Sturge Island was volcanic, bald, clean-shaven.

Since the death of his companions, Dan Yack had been living in a tent. He had elected to set up his dwelling in that same fault in the rock Ivan had once occupied, and there he had made a discovery.

He had found his own dinner-suit and, in the revolver-pocket of the trousers, a whole cache of monocles wrapped up in tissue paper.

So Billy, his model manservant, had not forgotten them. After counting and recounting them, Dan Yack threw the monocles into the sea.

And he put on his dinner-jacket and trousers.

He wore them every day, and it was in this outfit that he now made a tour of the island. Only once had he returned to the site of the house under the cliff. He had unearthed the famous crate containing the giant plum pudding and had been quite happy to find a crate of whisky bottles intact. The whisky was useful for washing in and he kept himself alive on three slices of plum pudding a day.

That was all.

He had no fire, no tobacco, and he lacked nothing! He desired nothing. He ate his plum pudding conscientiously, crumbling it in the palm of his hand, and solemnly washed himself from head to foot in whisky. He did not want to think of Hedwiga, so he railed at his beard to distract himself. He was very proud of his dinner-suit. The uniform of a civilized man. He did not feel that he was lost. He cleaned his nails with a flint. He was not waiting for anything.

Everything unfolded around him.

In calm and exceptionally clear weather a column of smoke rose very high in the air above the southern horizon. It was the plume of smoke from Mount Erebus.

Dan Yack never scanned the northern horizon, he never searched the seas in the hopes of seeing the ship arrive.

He was not on the look-out for anything.

It would have been unworthy of him.

He was sure of himself and knew how to wait.

Come what may.

And with everything at stake!

Although Dan Yack was not aware of it, the *Green Star* was making full steam towards him.

Summer was already on the wane.

Every day, garlands of crystals knotted and unknotted themselves on the thread of the water, and those curious formations of young ice that resemble the leaves of water-lilies – sailors call them 'pancakes' – drifted on the surface, growing denser and more compact day by day.

Everything was growing cold again and the sun was taking on a glassy, grainy look. The mists were thicker and it frequently snowed. The nights were rapidly drawing out.

Millions of iceberg fragments floated along the coast; they had all been worn away by the thaw and by their incessant movement in the sea; they took on bizarre and often elegant shapes, long swan-necks, fantastic crab claws, romantically entwined arms.

The thermometer was dropping slowly. The ship passed close to a towering iceberg that was like an immense fortress with turrets, loopholes and a Gothic arch; it gave off a kind of bluish, luminous aura.

The sea was heavy and choppy, in spite of the wind from the north-west.

Often the nights were gruelling; huge waves broke with great violence; the sea was 'scaly', as sailors say. But under storm-jib and deeply reefed canvas, and with a vigilant look-out to ensure that the ship weathered the buffeting of the sea, she made good progress and was not forced too far off her course.

The silence was absolute, imposing.

The seamen, navigating as if in the thraldom of a dream, were amazed by the architecture of the ice, which was in the outlandish styles of Magic City, Luna Park and the Alcazar; they were distracted by the slap of the waves against the ship, the heavy shocks of the water in the crevasses and grottoes, the crystalline murmuring of the ice, which moaned and let out unexpected sighs, the startling reverberations which suddenly echoed the familiar sounds of life on board ship, carrying them out to sea and bringing them back amplified, unrecognizable. Thus absorbed, the crew never gave a thought to all the possible dangers and the ship continued her zigzagging course in the colourful shadows of this strange labyrinthine world.

A huge whale swam within a few metres of the ship and, plunging like a plumb-line, left its tail-flukes sticking vertically out of the water for several seconds. They could see the shellfish clinging to it in great abundance, like barnacles on the hull of an old ship, and, with a roar of delight and a babble of rude remarks, the crew saluted the saffron-coloured excrement as the enormous creature, without the least trace of prudery, defecated into the water.

When the weather was calm and the sky cloudless, the stars shone with extraordinary brilliance.

Or, at times, it was the iceblink scintillating. A little later, the ship nosed its way into false pack-ice and navigation became an engrossing passion. They had to seek for the few open leads or the weak points in the ice; sometimes they attacked it by sheer force. They thrust through, capsizing great flat blocks of ice or riding over them so that the weight of the ship caused a fissure that widened into a serpentine channel and allowed them to pass through the obstacle. During these battles, the ship shuddered to the very truck of the mast and her hull made a cracking sound, but they got through nevertheless, leaving behind them a wake of spinning ice-floes, creaming and frothing, painted in all the beautiful greens of the glass-blower's art.

In his haste to reach his destination, Deene charged straight ahead. The captain of the *Green Star* was not in a good mood. The fishing so far had not been up to much and now, with this lousy job of fetching Dan Yack and his companions thrust upon him, he was afraid he would not get back before the close of the fishing season; if he arrived late, he would be forced to tack up and down the coast of Chile for a whole winter in order to make up a full cargo.

Deene's anger was constantly on the boil.

'When you have to deal with the bosses, and the bosses' sons, it's always the same old story,' he grumbled as he scanned the horizon. 'All the same, I'll be damned glad when we get there.'

'Full ahead!' he shouted from the mast-head, where he had perched himself the better to spy out his course.

'Full ahead!' repeated the man at the helm.

'Full stop!'

'Full stop!' repeated the helmsman.

'Engines astern!'

A collision. The bow lifted a little, then dropped down again. The ice-floe had passed.

'Full steam ahead!'

'Full steam ahead!' the man at the helm repeated calmly, while the wheel spun this way, then that, without rest or respite.

Around the large, wind-swept icebergs there is always a little open water which often extends for quite a distance and affords a passage that ends in a point. Naturally, sailors take advantage of these channels by shaving the sides of the great ice monsters as closely as possible; so transparent is the water at their feet that they can see the grottoes, the vaults and the submarine corridors which make up their enormous spurs.

On the morning of 3rd February the look-out has just called 'Land on the port bow!' when the weather becomes misty and a sort of half-melted snow begins to fall. Then the hurricane is unleashed, implacable, unforeseen, in all its violence and ferocity.

The sea is huge and seethes wickedly; the wind howls and the dense mist it drives before it falls on the men like a solid mass and seems to drag them along with it. The snow, in small, hard, compacted crystals, pierces the skin and eyes like packets of needles; the pain is unbearable and the effort of opening one's eyes, of trying to see clearly, is torture. The seaman at the helm, one of the bravest and hardiest, is weeping with misery, he bangs his poor swollen hands together furiously and stamps his feet, which are burning with cold. In the rosy glow of the binnacle-lamp, gleaming through the snow, one can make out his agonized face and the big teardrops furrowing his cheeks.

At the bow, the corpse of a seal is caught in the stays like the body of a sailor who has been flogged to death by the wind.

The greyish daylight surrounding the ship becomes denser and blacker, darkness falls. They can hear the sound of giant waves passing under the ship, lifting her up and covering her with spray that freezes instantly; for a few fractions of a second, they can make out their foaming crests as they rear up before disappearing once more into the darkness. The *Green Star* rises up, sinks down, lists, rises up again, breasting the heavy seas as best she can.

The barometer has dropped to 721.

4th February: the wind turns to the south-west and eases a little.

Deene takes advantage of this to come in nearer to the coast, which they have glimpsed through a clearing in the mist, but the weather remains overcast all day.

In the evening there is a slight lull, the night is relatively clear and, at sunrise, land can be descried, and Deene believes he recognizes certain familiar features. This must be Sturge Island.

5th February: once more the weather is overcast and grim; wind, snow, frozen pellets of snow and fog, a swelling sea; it is exhausting. Throughout the day and night they make for land, then head out to sea again. How long will this go on?

6th February: still the same. At 7 a.m., in an all-too-fleeting clearing, they see icebergs ahead. The ship goes about and the storm from the south-east recommences, even worse than before. Never has the wind blown with such force. The night that follows is arduous beyond all description.

7th February: dense fog, the wind drops, the ship is brutally shaken by growlers and can make no headway at all. Deene has not taken off his clothes for four days, he hasn't even pulled off his boots. The night is tolerable, but fog, squalls and snow persist.

8th February: towards three in the afternoon, the weather clears; little by little, the wind dies down; land is clearly visible. It is certainly Sturge Island. They can make out Mount Brown, then the face of the promontory. They must profit by the last of the daylight and try to reach the island before nightfall. The *Green Star* noses her way from iceberg to iceberg. Fortunately, the storm has dispersed the pack-ice. The slight wind that persists is a headwind and delays their progress, already slow because of the overdriven engines.

Night, black night, is coming on fast. The waves can be heard breaking against the reefs, astern, ahead, on all sides. Should they stop, go on, turn about?

Suddenly the silhouette of Mount Brown rears up against a luminous sky; a huge, pale but incandescent glow seems to emanate from it; the magnificently bright disc of the moon appears, transforming the giant menhir into an enchanted lighthouse. Everything around the ship is illuminated. The sea, the snow, the glaciers sparkle softly, like precious metals.

Slowly they enter the bay where the little port lies. Half an hour later they have moored the ship. The anchor looks totally deformed by the moonlight which adorns its flukes with alternately matt and shining ice.

Should they wait until daybreak in this unheard-of calm, which takes them by surprise, for by now they are so unaccustomed to it? No, in spite of the fact that everyone needs rest, Deene mans the whale-boat and has himself rowed ashore. The officer of the watch joyfully sounds the ship's siren and all the men who have remained on board cluster on deck to shout, at intervals, a resounding chorus: 'Ahoy! Three-Eyes, we're here! We're here!'

One of the men has a handbell, another a megaphone, still another a foghorn.

The weather is fine and cold.

The dawn is late in coming. To the north-east, two little round clouds are fringed with just the hint of a rainbow, a half-built bridge whose double arch spans a smoking cataract of green, violet and orange haze. The vault of the sky is utterly black and a resplendent azure band joins east to west. To the south, a gigantic fan opens up, a red and rose-coloured pillar of wind that disperses in the form of red ochre and dark blue cirro-stratus. The ocean is an immense circle of open water on whose surface icebergs float like wads of cotton wool.

The siren shrieks, the men on board shout. Deene and his crew have reached the site of the house under the cliff and are rummaging through the charred debris of the framework. They find nothing and not one of them has the courage to speak.

Dan Yack wakes up as usual. He hears the ship's siren and the shouts of seamen on board reach him from the distance. He is not surprised. He manifests no joy and is in no haste to leave his tent. On the contrary, he takes his time getting dressed, and it is only this special attention to his person, at such a moment, that betrays his anxiety. Deep down, he is troubled. While he is dusting down his dinner-jacket, he is asking himself, 'What the hell am I going to say to them?

'To speak - what torture, and what good will it do? What can I say?

'I shall have to offer them some explanations, but what explanations?

'—— Thank you, I am quite well. I assure you, gentlemen, nothing has happened to me, nothing in the least untoward.

'—— Good morning, Mr Deene. Good morning, Captain. Have you had a pleasant voyage?'

And so on and so forth.

Or else: 'I . . .'

What a shame, having to face his fellow-men once more.

He had been so happy, all alone.

Ah! . . .

He puts his head between his hands. He can feel his heart beating. He is compelled to sit down. Then he lies down again. No, he will not go out, never again. Never will he take the first step. They will have to come and get him.

Abruptly, he comes out of the tent. It takes every ounce of his energy.

What it costs him, this first step! And he's got his knife into Deene, he wishes he'd gone to hell.

He takes another step forward.

He is trembling in every limb.

The sky is empty, it is not yet time for the little snow petrel to appear, and there, at the foot of the promontory, amongst the shallows where the old female elephant seal comes to wallow and disport herself, the *Green Star* is riding gently at anchor.

Dan Yack braces himself so as not to weep. It is only now that he regrets having thrown away his monocles.

Three short blasts on the siren and a long hurrah make his head spin. The men on board have caught sight of him. Dan Yack does not know what is happening to him. He sees men coming out of the ruins of the house, running to meet him, then stopping, disconcerted. The captain detaches himself from a frosted backdrop, an immense, gesticulating silhouette that rushes to meet him, capering like a goat. Everything is spinning round. Roaring sounds split his skull, voices boom like thunder in his ears. Dan Yack puts up his hand and touches his cap.

'Good morning, Captain,' he says in a clear voice. 'Have you brought my mail?'

He is extrordinarily red in the face.

'Your . . .'

'Yes, my . . .'

'Your letters are on board. I thought . . .'

'That was a mistake. You should have brought them to me, Captain.'

He has spoken. He himself does not know what he has said. Faces form a circle round him, overlap, dilate, dozens of eyes leer out at him, wounding him, making his skin itch; they move away, come near again, like wasps, like needles of snow in a blizzard.

'So, Captain, let's go aboard,' he says, suddenly coming back to normal.

Dan Yack has the impression that someone has just slipped in behind him.

But there is no one behind him, nothing but the imprint of his own footsteps in the snow.

Dazed, he retraces them with his eyes. What a distance! What a long, long way he has come!

Never again will he enter that tent. No, never.

I've won the first round, he thinks all at once. Beware of the next!

'Well, shall we go?' he again asks Deene.

'But', says Deene hesitantly, 'aren't you bringing anything with you?'

'I have nothing.'

'And . . . and . . .' (Deene is more and more embarrassed) 'and . . . your companions?'

Dan Yack glances all round the faces that encircle him.

Only now does he recognize them. There is the old quartermaster with his quid of tobacco. That big red-headed fellow who looked after Bari on board. Batty, the ship's boy. And so many others, looking at him. And Deene. Deene in his natural shape and no longer gigantic as he seemed a moment ago, that poor little ship's master, Deene, who dandled him on his knee when he was a small boy.

Dan Yack blinks rapidly. He smiles.

'Well, boys, how goes it?'

And, addressing Deene: 'Shall we go on board, old man?'

Deene makes a sign to his men, Everyone embarks in the whale-boat and soon they are aboard the *Green Star*.

'Have you got a phonograph on board? All mine are lost,' says Dan Yack as he sets foot on deck.

. . . ?

'No? Well then, lend me your razor.'

And he goes below to his cabin.

'He's mad, you know,' Deene confides to his first mate.

'Possibly,' says the latter. 'I've reamed the pipes of the starboard boiler, the engine is ready.'

'Thank God for that,' say Deene. 'We'll be able to get under way tonight, the weather's set fair. Send as many men ashore as possible and get them to raise a cairn at the point of the promontory. Bloody hell, I'm turning in.'

And, growling as he goes: 'He's mad, I tell you, mad. What a bitch of a job!' he sighs as he gets back into his bunk.

In the cabin Dan Yack has stripped naked. Then, in feverish haste, he has shaved off his beard. Now he is contemplating himself in a mirror, from close to, as close as possible.

The miseries he has endured are plainly written on his face, but he has a determined and bloody-minded air about him.

He doesn't recognize his own expression, or his eye.

It is true that this is the first time he has seen himself without a monocle. For many years. What a victory! he thinks. But I must take care!

They have brought him his mail. Packets and packets of letters. And not one of them from Hedwiga.

Not one.

No, not a single, solitary one.

He could weep.

And, inside himself, he does weep, for a long time.

Without tears.

And with his eyes open.

Open on a world that is crumbling about him.

It doesn't matter, he thinks, it doesn't matter. I don't give a damn.

And he laughs.

The day elapses.

And the night.

In the morning he sends for the captain. For some time now, he has been aware that the ship is pitching heavily and the engine is making the partition behind his head vibrate. He is lying there with his eyes open, his mind emptied of thought.

'What does Hortalez want from me?' he asks Deene the moment he sets foot in the cabin.

And he shows him a dozen letters that have been forwarded from his London office, all bearing the heading of the Compañia Gonzalo Hortalez. 'What does he want from me?'

'Well, I don't know, sir.'

'Dan Yack!' thunders Dan Yack, furious. 'I've already told you my name is Dan Yack, Dan Yack, short and sweet, and that all the Williamses have gone, gone to the devil.'

'Yes, sir.'

'Dan Yack!' yells Dan Yack, beside himself.

Suddenly he calms down.

'Captain,' he says, 'set course for Chiloé, we're going to make whoopee.'

'But . . .'

'But me no buts, we're going to make whoopee, I tell you.'

Twenty-nine days later, the *Green Star* re-entered the normally frequented shipping channels and, for the first time in many long months, her navigation lights were lit at night.

Little Batty, whose duty it was to tend them, very proudly brought out the lamps he had polished especially for the occasion.

One red. One green. One white.

> Combs of wood,
> Tortoiseshell
> And polished horn,
> Split sleepers' eyes before the dawn.
> Gaiter-straps
> And ten-league boots
> Made from hide of pigs
> Cross mountains, buns and periwigs!
> And reach a happy land
> A mile above the sun
> Where kids play quoits with millstones
> While a corporal and three soldiers beat the sun with
> giants' bones.

The chief cook recited this nonsense rhyme by way of starting some cock-and-bull story amidst the smoke of many pipes.

In the fo'c'sle the men were laughing and joking, because they were on their way home, and soon there would be land.

Land for sailors!

A hundred years ago, Chiloé was a whalers' paradise where the homeward-bound seamen came to dance the fandango with the beautiful girls of San Carlos before sailing round Cape Horn; others came to refit in the midst of a voyage and to revictual with potatoes (an interesting detail: the potato originated in Chiloé) and lemons, when scurvy was making intolerable ravages amongst the crews. Today, in 1906, the town is sadly run down; it is called Ancud on account of its bishopric, its old Spanish cathedral, its seminary, its monasteries and convents, but, for the rest, there is nothing but a filthy barracks, a few stinking warehouses down on the waterfront (roofed with corrugated iron and erected in the name of progress), a single, lopsided street of old colonial houses, a suburb inhabited by fishermen and a whole jumble of straw huts, shanties and hovels, a pestilent zone that houses a floating population of wretchedly poor Indians who provide the casual labour for the exploitation of guano. The 'chilote' race is renowned for its intelligence and intellectuality, but, in the town, the inhabitants are divided into several castes according to the degree of their cross-breeding: Araucanian, Linare Puelche and Spanish. They do not mix with each other in any way, although they are all engaged in breeding fur-seals on behalf of two companies, one English and one German. There is a railway, still under construction, four or five newly painted, acetylene-lit bars, an Arab-style casino and a red-light district, but the lovely Chilean women who made San Carlos famous, and who were once the solace and delight of whalers, have well and truly deserted the place; in about 1850, at the time when gold was discovered in California, they took themselves off to embellish the whorehouses of San Francisco and they never came back. They have since been replaced by Basque women, who have settled and founded families, or by worn-out Patagonians and hideous shrews from Tierra del Fuego. Amongst these Magellanic women, the proudest, and the only beautiful ones (celebrated, moreover, for their impassivity and their cool, calculating shrewdness), are the daughters of the noble tribe of the Eoas; their fiancés, brothers and husbands willingly hire them out to the Europeans, considering it a matter of no consequence whatever, since the sailors passing through are ignorant of the use of the *guesquel*[6] and never manage to please their women; that is why the Eoas hold the Whites in profound contempt, cheat them for all they're worth and readily spill their blood when they happen to come across one, alone, sprawled on a *tarala* or bed of rushes, exhausted by his sexual excesses or sleeping off his wine in a hut. What a sailors' graveyard San Carlos

6   *guesquel*: see footnote on p. 116. – N.R.

is, and how many have gone missing there! What sinister tales are
whispered, fit to curdle a cabin-boy's blood!

In spite of this, and long before land was in sight, the crew of the
Green Star were already enjoying themselves.

> When all his pennies are
> Spent,
> It's time a whaler
> Went!

sang a wag. And God alone knew what sort of welcome awaited them
in this land they were approaching! In spite of the extreme south
latitude and the proximity of the great polar cold, everything one
discovers on arriving by sea - the mountains, the dells, the little,
isolated peaks, as well as the banks of the canals one sails up to reach
the anchorage between the islands - is covered in tropical forest. The
rain falls every day. The vegetation is magnificent and arborescent
ferns grow right down to the edge of the ocean. It is a veritable Eden
for eyes which have seen nothing but the sea for months on end. And
there are the perfumes of the shores, a sugary balm that blends with
the musty odours of the seal-breeding parks and with the idea of
women!

Dan Yack had asked the men: 'What would you most like to have
on shore?'

And, after a few hesitant confabulations, the answer had been
unanimous: 'A good booze-up!' As soon as the ship had been brought
to her berth, the anchors thrown out, the sails carefully clewed up, the
fires damped down, and the quarantine launch had shoved off after
making a health inspection, everybody went ashore. It was Dan Yack
who led the band and started the rounds of the bars. First, it was
Fulanita's, then The Spouting Whale, then Char à bancs, the
Hermosa Pesca, A la belle Nantaise, the New York Bar and, finally, the
Pourquoi Pépita?

There was bright sunshine that day. The *patrons* of the bars had
been told in advance that Dan Yack was footing the bill, so, wherever
they went, there was wine unlimited, wine, liqueurs, mixed drinks of
all kinds and in all proportions, drunk out of glasses of every shape
and size, bottles of every imaginable shape, and the rarest flagons,
which were the pride and joy of each particular bar, were taken down,
dusted off, emptied at a single draught, carried off and smashed

outside, beneath the naked feet of the curious onlookers.

What uproarious jokes! What a shindy, what a binge! And what a windfall for the women, who had never before taken part in such a lavish spree and who, for the first time ever, left their quarter in broad daylight to invade the only street in the town, the bars and the boutiques, where everything they fancied was bought for them, the whole raggle-taggle bunch of them all together, half-naked, growing ever more reckless and daring. Hadn't they taken it into their heads to lock up the sergeant in the *calabozo*, together with the five wretched soldiers who constituted the town's police force, and to liberate half a dozen flea-bitten Indians? An impromptu band of musicians had been scratched together and now they were dancing in the street, in couples, in heaps, in rounds, in gangs. All the layabouts, the stevedores, *los ladrones* and *los rateros*, formed an escort to the revelling sailors who were amusing themselves by getting the Indians they had sprung from the cooler drunk and carrying them off in triumph. What a crew of shady characters, but what a glorious booze-up!

Occasionally a girl would ask her sailor: 'But what are you celebrating, dearie, have you caught a sea monster?'

'Better than that, my beauty,' he would reply, 'we've fished up the boss's son.'

'That big fair-haired fellow who laughs all the time?'

'That's the one, that's our cherub!'

And the girl would timidly approach Dan Yack.

In fact, Dan Yack was letting rip like a pirate, but a good-natured pirate mollified by drink. He took no more notice of this girl than of the others. He was completely drunk and, little by little, he found himself all alone and feeling fragile. Then he amused himself all on his own, just as he had done as a child, lingering longer and longer in a bar after the others had left, squeezing the last exhausted drop of pleasure out of everything, right up to the moment when the overworked machines – the phonographs, the stereoscopic views, the automatic rifle, the standing figure of the boxer and a game that involved a monstrous massacre – broke down. He never had enough small change and kept yelling his head off for coins or counters. While they were changing a large banknote for him, he took advantage of the lull to drink and ponder on some means by which he could cheat the penny-in-the-slot machines. He wanted to win, to win at every throw, to win for certain, that is to say, to ensure that the machine, once triggered off, would never stop. A typical drunkard's notion, and what a party he was having! Immediately he began feeding money into the slots again, doubling, tripling the stakes, pulling on the handle, holding it down or letting it go abruptly, giving it a sly shove, trying to demolish the machine; in a word, having the time of his life.

The star turn of all these automata was to be found in the Pourquoi Pépita?, and every quarter of an hour the insatiable Dan Yack ran back there, into the bar, to set this masterpiece of human ingenuity in motion. It was a pneumatic machine, registered and patented in every country in the world by the Gebrüder Fugger, Münster, Germany, according to the declaration on the maker's trade mark, which was framed by a whole rigmarole of gold medals, two *grands prix* at the Expositions Universelles, Paris 1878 and Paris 1889, *hors concours* and special jury prize, etc. etc. It was a mechanical orchestra, composed of stuffed cats mounted on an endless cable which activated them, made them move, open their eyes, nod their heads, wave their paws and play like real musicians seized with St Vitus's dance. And with what *furia* they played the piece and, once the peso had slipped into the slot, what a caterwauling was unleashed! The conductor of the orchestra, a big, black, ungainly Tom, suddenly threw an epileptic fit and beat time furiously. The trumpeter trumpeted, the fiddler fiddled, the drummer was a veritable virtuoso of flurry and flourish. Two dear little white she-cats, two dancers dressed in tutus with pink ribbons round their necks, jigged up and down on their spiral spring and, at the end of each piece, a little bird popped out of its glass cage, hopped on to the conductor's music-stand, warbled a little tune, fluttered its wings and swiftly returned to its cage; then, by way of a finale, the instrument erupted in a mighty fart of diabolical miaowings. God it was marvellous, astonishing, unimaginable and yet real! Dan Yack was ready to spend his entire fortune on it!

Ah, if only he could procure this automaton! He questioned the *patron*, wrote down the manufacturer's address, had them explain the workings of the apparatus to him, made them open it up, looked inside to see that was in its innards and started it up again, making it play incessantly.

Every piece. The whole repertoire.

He was in raptures.

And it was there, that evening, that he was finally joined by a little man as round and jovial as a Valencia orange.

Just then, the cats' orchestra was playing 'Les Cloches de Corneville'.

And behind the jovial little man came Deene.

What fun it was!

Deene looked surlier and more worried than ever, and the little round jovial man bowed and scraped, bobbing up and down several times, clicking his heels and saying rapidly: 'Dan Yack' (Deene must have been coaching him), 'Dan Yack, allow me to introduce myself. I am Hortalez, Gonzalo Hortalez junior, from the Compañía Gonzalo Hortalez of Punta Arenas. It was I who wrote to you. I have come all the way from London, where I must return, especially to seek you out. I have a very interesting proposition to put to you on behalf of our company.'

Dan Yack burst out laughing.

'Well, what do you want of me?'

But he did not give him a chance to speak. The instrument had not yet finished its miaowings before Dan Yack slipped another coin into the apparatus and the cats' orchestra struck up the Wedding March from *Lohengrin*, con brio.

'Sit down. Isn't this magnificent? What will you have to drink? If it were mine, I'd have them all dressed up. Waiter, a bottle of champagne and some caviare! What do you think of my idea of having little black suits made for them by Meyer and Mortimer's in London, since, at the moment, my cats are a little shabby? Deene, did the men go back on board this evening? No? Well, that's all right. I'd like to electrify this machine, then it would never stop. Well now, what are they saying about me in London?'

And again Dan Yack burst out laughing. Then, insolently, he looked Hortalez up and down, taking stock. He had completely forgotten that he was no longer wearing a monocle . . .

'Ah, these cats! . . .'

And he laughed again.

'Come along, let's have dinner,' said Dan Yack.

And they went to the casino to dine.

As he stood up, Dan Yack upset the table and broke all the champagne glasses.

'Never mind,' he said, laughing louder than ever. 'It's plain glass, and that brings good luck.'

Dan Yack had just broken the bank. He came up to Hortalez junior, his hands brimming with loot, banknotes spilling out of his pockets and scattering in a trail behind him.

'Well,' he asked him, 'do you still want to try your luck? I'm on a winning streak tonight, you know.'

'All right,' Hortalez replied. 'Sit down.'

Deene looked at him, dumbfounded.

There was no orchestra in the room. This was no Monte Carlo; here in San Carlos roulette was played on a long table covered with American cloth on which the numbers, framed in rectangles, had been painted a dingy yellow. A croupier spun a portable roulette wheel which pointed to the winning number. A heteroclite crowd surrounded this long table as well as the one where they were playing *chemin de fer* and the little baccarat table Dan Yack had just quitted. It was strictly men only in this Moorish-style room, pompously entitled the Grand Saloon, and, as every one of them was smoking, the dense smoke of cigars obscured the four ostrich eggs hanging from the ceiling, one in each corner, suspended in horsehair nets like the eye of God in the clouds. Long knives made the gamblers' jackets bulge at the hip, and now and then, as the croupier moved about, the butt of a revolver could be glimpsed protruding from his pocket.

'Let's get out of here,' said Dan Yack. 'Let's go back to the Pourquoi Pépita? I'm bored here. We can play some music and you can tell me your story.'

All three of them stood up, but Deene did not want to go with them. His eyes were starting out of his head and he was red in the face. He had drunk too much and, above all, had had far too much to eat.

'Follow your men's example,' Dan Yack said to him as they were leaving, 'don't go back on board tonight.'

Deene gave him a grateful smile; he was finally reassured - the excellent dinner and the baccarat game had convinced him that Dan Yack wasn't mad, And, ah, what a game it had been! He took a few tottering steps and, for the first time in his life, risked ten pounds sterling on the roulette table, but he didn't bother to wait and find out whether he had lost or won, he made straight for the private rooms upstairs. There was a staircase to be climbed and, at the top, in a kind of hanging stage-box, some naked women were reclining on a red sofa. These women gave him the glad eye.

'I'm going up,' said Deene, clutching the banister rail with both hands.

And he climbed the treacherous staircase, stumbling, dazzled, as if he were ascending Jacob's ladder.

As soon as he arrived at the Pourquoi Pépita? Dan Yack ordered oysters and cocktails. He had brought with him a little barefoot urchin, picked up in the streets, and now he gave him a pile of silver coins and told him to keep feeding them into the music-machine.

'Well now, I'm listening,' said Dan Yack to Hortalez as the orchestra started up, furiously. 'Do you hear my cats? I'm all ears. What have you got to say to me?'

The cats' orchestra was playing 'The Postilion of Longjumeau'.

Marvellous!

Dan Yack rocked back and forth in his chair.

'Well now, tell me, what do you want?'

'I want to buy your island,' said Hortalez, gulping down one of those plump oysters that are the speciality of Chiloé.

'Which island?'

'The one you've just come from.'

Dan Yack burst out laughing.

'You want to buy my island? But do you know what there is on my island, Hortalez?'

'All right, all right,' said Hortalez, laughing. 'But don't try to pull a fast one on me, Dan Yack, we have made inquiries.'

'You've made inquiries?' (Dan Yack couldn't get over it). 'And what have you learned from your inquiries?'

'They are saying in London,' Hortalez replied, 'they say you've discovered a . . .'

'I don't want to hear what you've learned from the Schimmelpfennig Agency in London,' Dan Yack interrupted. 'Will you gamble with me, my island against . . .'

'Against a fifty per cent share in the profits of our company,' Hortalez junior gravely proposed.

'Ah, so that's what you're after,' observed Dan Yack mockingly.

Hortalez junior bit his lip.

'A *zanzi*?' asked Dan Yack.

'A *zanzi*,' Hortalez agreed.

Dan Yack had the dice brought to him in a shaker and ordered another round of cocktails.

'I bet you've lost,' said Dan Yack, turning the leather goblet upside-down on the table. 'Look, a *zanzi* of aces. And now, would you like to know what there is on my island?'

'Tell me,' said the crestfallen Hortalez.

'An old female elephant seal, and that's all. I'll give you a chance to get your own back.'

'And to think that everyone in London imagines you've discovered new fishing grounds!' exclaimed Hortalez. 'It's impossible, a *William*? But what did you go down there for?'

'That's my business,' replied Dan Yack. '*Primo*, my name is Dan Yack, just that, no more William, and, *secundo*, I went down there for fun.'

'For fun?' reiterated an incredulous Hortalez.

Dan Yack rocked in his chair and smiled at Hortalez. The cats' orchestra never stopped, the little guttersnipe did his duty conscientiously and was so interested in his work that he was even doing his utmost to imitate the antics of the cats, who were playing *Carmen*. It was perfect, all it lacked now was an Italian tenor.

'For fun?' reiterated Hortalez. 'But do you know, Dan Yack, that our business is doing very badly, the industry has gone to pot! A new society has been formed, in competition with our two trusts, the Norwegians made seven million crowns out of their catch last summer! But didn't you read my letters, then?'

'No, I tore them up,' Dan Yack admitted naïvely.

'Hell's teeth and buckets of blood! Our goose is cooked, then!' said Hortalez, bounding out of his chair. 'But, Dan Yack, we were counting solely on you, on an understanding between our two companies – just think, seven million crowns in their first year! We can no longer fight them alone, it would eat up all our capital, I wanted to make you a proposition . . .'

'You can tell me all that later,' said Dan Yack, laughing. 'Calm down, my friend, and don't pull such a long face, what the hell! Don't you find it exciting, all this you're telling me? And don't forget I've offered you a chance of revenge, another game of *zanzi* if you like? We'll play . . . we'll play . . . well, what the devil shall we play for? Listen, we could play for fifty per cent. . . . No, perhaps not. . . . Do you know how I passed my time on the island?'

'. . . ?'

'Practising throwing dice. I can throw a *zanzi* of aces at every throw. So you would be bound to lose. Tell me, Hortalez, do you like reading?'

'No, why?'

'Then you're like me, I never open a book. So you're not familiar

with the story of the prisoner who trained spiders in his cell? He was
serving a life sentence and the spiders came and told him what the
weather was like outside. And do you know why he trained these
spiders? It's a riddle that somebody asked me one day.'

'No, why?'

'Ah, I thought you were smarter than that, my friend. It was to kill
time, of course. As for me, during my stay down there, I amused
myself and killed time by trying to train chance. You know, I'm in
training now, in good form, and I have the necessary sleight-of-hand.
Tell me, how many ships have you got?'

'Seventy.'

'I have a hundred and twenty. I'll sell them to you.'

'What, sell them?' expostulated Hortalez.

'Yes, my dear fellow,' said Dan Yack. 'We should not make a
merger of our two companies. Everything must be liquidated, we
must go bankrupt, blow up the whole caboodle, clear the decks, start
again from scratch. I am delighted to have made your acquaintance,
Hortalez.'

'But you're mad!' Hortalez exclaimed in spite of himself. 'Oh,
excuse me,' he added, blushing crimson.

But the word had slipped out.

'Yes, so Captain Deene believes,' admitted Dan Yack. 'It is also true
that I'm not too sure what I'm saying just at this moment, but don't
worry, I have an idea. And I have too much business sense - a lousy
family heritage, you know - not to realize that one never visualizes
things on a big scale, no, never big enough, at the start of a new
enterprise, especially after an early success, and that's where we shall
beat your Norwegians at their own game. They are not thinking so
much of the whales as they are of ruining us, and we're going to throw
them the bait, the bait of our fleets, our old equipment, all our
experience, even our time-honoured fishing concessions, which are
fished out. What a terrific deal we can make! Tell me, what's the
average age of your boats, fifty?'

'Not so old as that, thirty or forty.'

'Mine are over seventy years old, on average. Yet another
inheritance from the family, you see, built of teak, indestructible, and
yet another reason for getting rid of them. You don't cling to yours for
sentimental reasons, do you? We must modernize, move with the
spirit of the times. Our generation has to start everything all over again.
What the old folks did was good, but it's too restricted for us. They

were always held back by all sorts of considerations of honour, wealth and respectability, and besides, they always shut the door behind them. With us, where one man forces his way through, the whole world must rush in behind, isn't that what you believe, too? Business isn't just business, it's whatever we wish it to be - our adventures, our loves, our desires, our thoughts, our most obscure needs, our craziest dreams. Are you yourself very keen on money? And aren't you bored stiff? And longing to enjoy yourself, that is to say, to destroy, create, succeed, fail? In short, do something new and amusing, with no ulterior motive other than the desire to exploit the present moment, which is ever-changing, uncertain, fugitive and yet as forceful as an explosive? Don't you always long to put a match to the gunpowder? If not, why did you come here and seek me out? It wasn't only to set your company on its feet again, I believe, since you've been telling me all about the Norwegians. You want to fight, don't you, eh? Risk the whole shebang? Take a chance, isn't that it, huh? Tell me, Hortalez, was it your board of advisers who sent you to me, or did you come off your own bat?'

'Oh,' said Hortalez, 'we don't have a board of advisers, at most a family council and that's it! Our business is perfectly safe and reliable. It's generally the oldest member of the family who makes all the important decisions. So, since my father's death, responsibility for the whole enterprise rests on my shoulders. Moreover, I didn't need to consult anyone else before taking the initiative and coming to find you. I . . .'

'Just as I thought!' cried Dan Yack. 'Well then, since you've already had the courage to come to me and try to put an end to the ancient rivalry between our two companies, listen to my advice: put the whole caboodle on the market, including the reputation and high standing of your firm. Here, let me shake you by the hand, I like you, and your Norwegians will sink without trace. You've had enough of being a daddy's boy, eh? I know how you feel, I don't even want to be known by my family name any more! Listen, in everybody else's eyes, I am never anything but the boss's son, even nowadays, when I'm the sole boss, I'm still the son - in other words, incapable, impotent, a lucky devil cashing in on a situation created by others, a lazy booby enjoying his daddy's fame and fortune, always his daddy's. Very well then, yes, I am a man who enjoys his pleasures, but I'm going to show them what I'm capable of. I'll chuck everything to the four winds and put all my personal fortune into this new enterprise. Follow me,

Hortalez, or rather, march by my side. I'll stake everything on a single card. You did the right thing by coming to see me, Hortalez, and those Norwegians of yours had better hang on tight. You tell me our industry is ruined, but I tell you it isn't even born yet! Look out, take cover! I'm going to show them what the whaling industry can produce nowadays. And, of course, these Norwegians of yours are well equipped?'

'Oh, as to that,' cried Hortalez warmly, 'they are marvellously fitted out! They have a fleet of small steamers, all made of steel, each about forty tons, specially built for whale-catching in the Antarctic regions, wonderfully easy to manoeuvre, very fast, and they can ride out the heaviest seas and the worst kind of weather. Naturally the Norwegians only hunt with cannons, but the novelty is that their harpoon is automatic, it fires like a torpedo. When it strikes the whale, the two flukes of the harpoon separate and detonate a small shell of asphyxiating gas. The animal's corpse is then recovered with a steam-winch, it is secured alongside and, to prevent its sinking, it is inflated by means of a large hollow lance connected to the air-pump, then it's towed back to the whaling-station. It seems that a single one of these little boats can come back with as many as three, and sometimes even six, whales.'

'And that is what amazes you?' said Dan Yack. 'But, my dear fellow, it was a French invention, one that our company never wanted to put into practice – family pride again, reinforced by questions of national honour, not wanting to be outdone by foreigners. It was the invention of a certain Monsieur Devisme, from Nantes, whose harpoon was tipped with prussic acid, or something of the sort. We have had his dossier in our archives since 1877. The projectile penetrates the blubber, bursts through it, divides and, in some way, attacks the whole cavity of the thorax, perforating, lacerating, tearing and destroying the vital organs. To all these wounds, all these causes of death, must be added asphyxia or blood-poisoning from the carbon monoxide which is released by the combustion of the powder, or by the prussic acid which leaks out. We never took this invention seriously. All the same, those Norwegians have got a nerve, inaugurating such a novel method, and they were lucky to obtain such fine results from the very first blow. But we'll do better than that, the two of us, you'll see. Tell me, Hortalez, what areas have they been operating in this summer?

'Their centre of operations was in Port Deception.'

'In the South Shetlands? But that was my great-grandfather's fishing rendezvous! There's been nothing there for a long time now, since the famous slaughter of the fur-seals, and more particularly, no right whales.'

'That's correct, but there are schools of rorqual,' Hortalez replied. 'As they've never been hunted, there are rorquals, humpbacks, finbacks and minkes in profusion. And that's the real revolution these blessed Norwegians have brought about, they attack all the bottom-dwelling species, as they can inflate them after capture to prevent them sinking. Moreover, they have a factory ship anchored at the entrance to Port Deception which dissects and grinds everything to powder, working flat out, without a break, all through the summer. God, what a mess!'

'My word, that's a bit much,' declared Dan Yack.

'Oh yes, it's a perfect scandal!' said Hortalez, flying into a temper. 'It seems the bay was full of disembowelled carcases, piles of them right up to Pendulum Cove. If any boat had come in to seek a haven there during bad weather, it wouldn't have been able to get in to shelter! It's . . .'

'Waiter, a bottle of liqueur brandy!' shouted Dan Yack. 'There's nothing like it', he confided to Hortalez, 'for freshening up your ideas when you've had a drop too much to drink. Taste it, you'll see. This brandy is as good as a night's sleep, or a day of calm reflection. My plan is all drawn up and your Norwegians will swallow it, hook, line and sinker. What a lark! We're going to have a good time! Listen, give me your pen and some paper, I'm going to lay the foundations of the S.B.C. Ltd, the *Sociedad Ballenera Chilotes* - is that the correct way to say it in Spanish?'

He drank six glasses of brandy, one after the other, then went on: 'Headquarters, London. Home port, San Carlos-de-Ancud, a joint-stock company with limited liability. But, good God, what's happened to the music?' thundered Dan Yack. 'Hey, littl'un, what the hell are you up to?'

The child was asleep. The orchestra had fallen silent some time ago. In the end the mechanism had broken down and the cats, surprised by the abrupt ending of the music, had frozen, some with one paw in the air, some brandishing their instruments, another with his muzzle leaning on his violin or with his flute applied to his eye, ridiculous and striking, like the cadavers of the Romans unearthed at Pompeii, still attending to their various occupations or their pleasures, one kneading dough, another making love, each fixed in the gesture or in the grimace he was making at the moment when the cataclysm suffocated him, even before he had had time to be startled or feel afraid. Like them, the cats had moved for perhaps another ten-millionth of a second, which was why they all looked so dislocated.

'Hey! Littl'un!'

But Dan Yack didn't have the heart to wake the child who was sleeping peacefully.

'*Patron*,' he said, tiptoeing up to the bar, 'you let rooms, don't you? I want to book the lot. I prefer not to have neighbours, so turn out all your lodgers, if you've got any, and tomorrow morning you can send for my luggage, it's on board, and it's not heavy! I'm staying with you for six months, try and repair your orchestra as quickly as possible, will you? If not, I'm moving out. Now, tuck this ragamuffin into a bed for me, and do it gently, don't wake him up. Wait, I'll come up with you. Hortalez, drink up the brandy, I'll be back in a second.'

Hortalez did not touch the liqueur brandy, for he had already drunk too much. He waited a long time. He was slightly dazed. Is it the alcohol or is it that idiot, Dan Yack? He wondered. In any case, he's a character.

He was almost nodding off.

Normally Gonzalo Hortalez junior was only too lively, he moved about a great deal, talked a lot, was very excitable and had so much surplus energy that he didn't know how to work it all off. Often he wasted his energy without rhyme or reason. He was a glutton for work. In his offices in Punta Arenas they had nicknamed him St Vitus.

Like many Latins who are talkative, intelligent and hyperactive, Hortalez had a fundamentally passive mind. Latins easily fall into a routine, almost always as a matter of convenience. Nine times out of ten it is simply out of opportunism that they become enterprising and optimistic; they have plenty of time ahead of them, since they come from a very ancient race, and their joviality more often than not hides a mental apathy, a lack of ideas. They like the easy life, which is why they are traditionalists, in spite of all their fine inventions. Though they express them passionately, their unconventional ideas never break through into the realm of action; they are the last flowering of classical rhetoric, of verbalism, pure complaisance towards oneself, a kind of aerophagy; it is only the Anglo-Saxon who deliberately throws himself into the absurd and acts without wasting time or losing his equilibrium, yet he is considered to be a practical man, and the Latin admires him for it.

Hortalez did not yet admire Dan Yack; he was, rather, frightened of him.

He is uneducated, he thought, and he drinks too much.

He's mad, but he sees things clearly.

What should I do?

Hortalez was beginning to worry.

'Why did I come here?' he asked himself.

The bar was deserted.

Hortalez yawned.

He was fed up with waiting.

His head was spinning.

He felt limp.

'What the hell is he doing up there?

'I've had too much to drink.'

Time passed.

Dan Yack did not return.

So Hortalez went upstairs. He saw light under one of the doors. He went in without knocking. Dan Yack was writing by the light of a candle that had burned low and, through the open window, there came the frantic chirping of birds. The dawn chorus.

'Excuse me,' said Dan Yack, 'I've just finished. Here's my power of attorney, a contract of partnership, the acts of assignment and sale. Sign them, we have all day to get them registered and legalize these papers at a notary's and at the consulate. You will leave this evening with Deene, you will sail on the first boat out of Buenos Aires. Here's my plan of action and my instructions, you'll have time to study the whole thing on board ship. Ah! You won't have time to get bored in Europe.'

'And you?'

'I shan't be bored either, I'll be up to my ears in work. I'm staying here for six months to take delivery, then, in the spring, I'll leave to supervise the installation of the factory at . . .'

'What factory?'

'A reinforced concrete factory, my dear fellow, which will be built at the entrance to Port Deception, at the very spot where your Norwegians moor their factory ship. They'll look a bit sick when they see we've ousted them. A permanent factory which will work night and day, winter as well as summer.'

'During the winter?'

'Yes, in the summer it will exploit the catch and in the winter we shall recover the by-products. So, nothing will be wasted, we shall salvage it all, you understand, every scrap of it. We'll make ropes out of the flippers, clothes out of the skin and tendons, and linoleum out of the guts.'

'Linoleum?'

'Exactly, linoleum. I bought the patent some time ago. Take this, it's a letter of introduction to the inventor. Do your best to send him to me quickly, he's a first-rate chemist, he'll be invaluable to us. His name is Herr Doktor Sch——'

'But what will you do with the bones?'

'The bones? Break them up, grind them to powder and make glue and fertilizer out of them.'

'Oh, you're very sure of yourself, aren't you?'

'On the contrary! For the moment, we must question everything, because now all things are possible. I've even thought of making canned foods.'

'Canned whalemeat? Impossible!'

'And why not? According to the Eskimos, the flesh of the fin-back tastes like sturgeon. What a market we'd have, if we managed to launch this product and persuade the army to include it as a staple item in rations! It's a complete food. You must try to sell the idea to European governments.'

'You are an extraordinary man!' cried Hortalez, carried away.

'Well then, is it a deal?'

'It's a deal.'

'Done!' said Dan Yack, holding out his hand.

The two men laughed.

'What time is it?' asked Dan Yack. 'I'd like to send a cable that will really pull the rug from under the feet of your Norwegians. Tough luck! Shit, if they knew what was coming to them!'

'What are you going to do?'

'I'm going to ask the Admiralty for a ninety-nine-year concession, exclusive fishing rights in the South Shetlands. By this evening I'll have the concession in my pocket, and for a peppercorn rent. They can't refuse my request in London. The South Shetlands are English, and I'm English, so . . .'

'Ach, that's outrageous!' cried Hortalez.

'Yes, it's outrageous,' said Dan Yack, 'and you would never have thought of it.'

'Never in my life. I thought the Shetlands . . .'

'They've been British since the days when my great-grandfather was there. For once, my family has come in useful. Let's get down to the telegraph office.'

But, before leaving, Dan Yack bent over the bed. The little barefoot urchin he had picked up in the street was sleeping there. He was stark naked, dirty and beautiful amongst the rumpled sheets. He must have been tossing and turning in his sleep and he was smiling as if still listening to the cats' orchestra. Dan Yack pulled up the covers, tucked the boy in and, taking all the money he had won at baccarat that evening, he stuffed it into the bed – fistfuls of banknotes under the pillow, under the boy's armpits, between his arms, between his legs, wherever there was a hollow to be filled.

'He's my mascot,' he murmured, 'I think I've won the second round.'

'What's that you say?' asked Hortalez, intrigued by these goings-on.

'Nothing,' replied Dan Yack, smiling. 'You know, I talk to myself sometimes. Let's go.'

It was wet outside. Heavy rain was already falling and the birds had ceased to sing. Dan Yack clung to Hortalez's arm. He was dead tired.

'I don't think I've forgotten anything,' he explained mechanically. 'I've ordered tons of equipment. You must make all your moves very secretly. No word of our new partnership must leak out. I shall wait here till the first boats arrive. Perhaps it would be as well if you went to Chicago to order the machinery for the factory, then it can be modelled on the ones they use in the abattoirs there. I am hoping to be ready to leave a good two months before the regular whaling fleet, it's a matter of organization and luck – the luck I already have, and I shan't let go of it. Take out a subscription to a meteorological service for me. You'll have to go to Germany, too, nobody but the Germans will come into these remote latitudes to refuel ships . . .'

He talked and talked, and already he had lost interest in the whole business. It seemed to him that the game was already won. Dan Yack had the impression that he was dealing with a man of straw, someone who was temporarily out of the game, like the dummy at whist or bridge.

The two men paced up and down outside the telegraph office, waiting for the counter to open.

At last, just as Dan Yack was in the process of sending his cable to William Aspinwall, Lord Bradley of the Admiralty, a great hullabaloo started up in the street. Dan Yack rushed to the window. It was the crew of the *Green Star* returning to the ship, tattered and torn, dog-tired, a disorderly rabble with the stragglers dropping like ninepins into every puddle. The men were singing, singing their heads off; it was a folk-song, one of those silly, sentimental sea-shanties that are quite meaningless but make you laugh with distress and fatigue.

> Tell us, children, where are our arms?
> Our arms are with our wives.
>
> Tell us, children, where are our wives?
> Our wives are with our arms.
>
> Tell us, children, etc. etc.

'Ah, my fine fellows!' exclaimed Dan Yack, suddenly restored to life. 'I expect I'll have a huge bill to pay, and I bet they've done plenty of damage!'

And so began for Dan Yack an absurd and delicious life which lasted for six months, the whole duration of his stay in San Carlos. Never had he been so happy and never before had he had so much fun.

Everything he did was so spontaneous and topsy-turvy that his life seemed to have something of the miraculous about it, and all his days were filled with precious moments, as if he were living a fairy-tale in which everything turned to his advantage and tirelessly renewed itself.

Yet there was nothing eccentric about his behaviour.

On the contrary, he did the same things every day, at the same time and in the same fashion.

As he had got drunk on his first day, Dan Yack continued to booze heavily; as he had heard the birds on his first morning, Dan Yack went out before dawn every day to walk in the hills; as he had set up a new business, Dan Yack continued to send cables every day at the same time and from the same counter, indeed his punctuality became legendary and they could have set the clock in the telegraph office by the moment of his arrival there; he continued making the cats' orchestra play and creating havoc day and night in the bar of the Pourquoi Pépita? But what turned his life completely upside-down and gave it an undreamed-of savour, allowing him to discover riches of sensation beneath its apparent monotony, was an acquired habit, the use of the *guesquel.**

It was thanks to an indiscretion on the part of little José-Pinto that Dan Yack had found out about the use of this sexual instrument.

José-Pinto was the guttersnipe he had picked up in the street and stuffed with money. Since then, the child had never left his side. He took his duties as factotum seriously. He continued to set the cats' orchestra in motion, during the afternoons and very late at night, and Dan Yack continued to stuff him with money, only now he gave him gold coins and José-Pinto brought him the most beautiful girls from the Eoas tribe. The kid was sharp-witted and taciturn, a smooth-tongued wheedler. He followed Dan Yack like a dog.

'How splendid life is, and nothing takes you out of yourself like a new sensual pleasure!' Dan Yack reflected.

He was hopelessly at sea, as one always is when the chance comes along to satisfy a long-repressed desire naturally. He, who so loved to give people pleasure, and whose kindnesses were always misinterpreted!

His heart was touched by these anonymous Indian women who allowed him to give them pleasure.

---

* The *guesquel* is an instrument used by the Patagonian Indians to pleasure their women. It consists of a little crown of tufts, made out of mule-hair, carefully mounted on a fine tricolour thread. The man attaches this thread behind the glans and during coitus he introduces the instrument, bristles foremost, into the woman's vagina. These tufts are stiff and at least as long as a finger; their effect is so violent that the woman cries out, weeps, grinds her teeth, bites, bursts out laughing, sobs, tosses, foams at the mouth, slobbers, twitches and writhes her hips (this is why the Patagonians call white women *corcoveadores*: because they do not need the *guesquel* to stimulate them, but take an active part in the love act and writhe naturally, to the delight of the men); the orgasm is so powerful that, after detumescence, the woman remains exhausted, at her last gasp, sated, replete, overcome, dizzy with happiness, stupefied to the point of tears and utterly helpless. It is claimed that, once they have experienced it, the Indian women cannot do without it, even in marriage, and that a good *guesquel* is worth three to six horses, according to the skill and care that have gone into its making, the abundance of the bristles, the quality of the mule-hair and the patterns, blue, white and red, of the thread; some of them end in little bunches of shells that tintinnabulate between the testicles during coitus, and this, they say, stimulates the man. The most sought-after are those made with the hair of a white mule because great prophylactic qualities are attributed to them.

The Patagonians make a great mystery of this instrument and women are forbidden to pronounce its name on pain of being repudiated, or even chased out of their tribe.

Without shame.

A cruel joy, but a joy.

And such emotion!

He drank several glasses of brandy in quick succession and began drafting more cables. Alcohol made him lucid and daring and sharpened his already keen nose for a speculation. Sitting at his table, by the light of a miserable candle, Dan Yack consulted his Bentley code. At the far end of the room, in the large, rumpled Spanish bed, the Indian woman whom he had been labouring over throughout the entire latter half of the night, was writhing, moaning and happy, her body still contorted by shudders of delight or arched by the cramps, or, on the other hand, lying inert and with her limbs slack. With her damp belly, her overflowing heart, her bursting throat, she burrowed down into the bed, sighing out a whole litany of weary and troubled words in a minor key. They were words of love. Many were disyllabic and all were profoundly musical and curiously stressed, the phrases full of doublets, like the trilling of certain birds.

> MAI-MAI—CARA-CARA—CACA—
> CACA—MOU-TCHI.

I love you (more than anything). I want (absolutely) my (which belongs to no one else) big male.

> IABOA CHARCOT FOUZKAOOS
> JYLONEXWEY

CIRCUMVENT MEMBERS OF CHARCOT EXPEDITION STOP OBTAIN FURTHER INFORMATION, wrote Dan Yack, consulting his telegraphic code.

> MINCHIMAUIDA—RUCULHUEN—
> RUCUL—TATA-TATA-POO-OO-CUM.

Hail, all Hail to Thee (Thee, divinity), love (great voluptuous delight) again, enough, I can bear no more (never more), I (to you),

the Indian woman went on.

> JILUBEIZLA AJAURWKALE EXE-
> GNIZZMA

BEAR ALL WHALING INDUSTRY SHARES.

BIHYOVEPZO WISAZDIZIF AHZYK-
GUBRO COFRA HEAVERS ENGKE

GET CONTRACTUAL MONOPOLY ALL AVAILABLE GERMAN COLLIERS, Dan
Yack telegraphed to Hortalez.

TAROSHEHUEN-TARO—QXI-QXII-I

*Great fish that penetrates (God who swims in), he who is the
Creator of All, All and I with him (participating therein).*

The dawn was breaking. Dan Yack got up, intending to go out. He
bent once more over the Indian woman who lay in his bed purring, in a
kind of delirium that was gently subsiding into sleep.

He leaned over the naked woman.

He greatly admired these daughters of nature whose skin shone like
burnished brass.

Their foreheads were tattooed with a star. A band of red wool
encircled their black hair, and bizarre blue lines decorated their
breasts and shoulders.

'What a discovery!' said Dan Yack to himself, thinking of the
astounding effects of the *guesquel* and listening to the cooing of the
ecstatic Indian woman.

'It's almost as beautiful as my record of the sea-lion,' he added as he
left the room.

He went out in a pensive mood.

And since, in an excess of gratitude, he never took off the *guesquel*
he wore, the shells tinkled like sleigh-bells at every step: *Gling-
glinggling-crakataka-gling.*

He walked in a dream.

The few half-castes who were on their way to work at this early
hour of the morning turned round, intrigued, as he passed. José-Pinto
followed him at a distance.

Dan Yack climbed up into the hills. The farther he left the coast
behind him, the more he discovered nature in her virgin state. The
birds flew more fearlessly, the pigeons no longer took flight at the
sound of his footsteps and the tree runners, hidden in thickets of
acacia, never ceased to pour their melodious warbling into the nascent

dawn. Always dressed in black, shot with brilliant blue reflections, and with a gorget of white feathers at its throat, curled and silky like a pleated and embroidered cravat, this bird was well named *toui-toui* in the native tongue, for it commenced all its calls with this first motet: *toui-toui, touitouitouitoui, toui.*

At intervals amongst the trees, the trunks of *nahuelhuelpis*, immense podocarps, lay on the ground, dismasted by their great age. The wreckage of these giant trees was always surrounded by a clearing. Pines and plantains in the vicinity were exposed to view, so it was easy for carnivores to take their fill of the pigeons in their branches. The pigeons of Chiloé are magnificent. When they shelter amongst the foliage, a white breastplate betrays them to the keen eyes of the hunter, and their throats are more like shot silk than the iridescent material of that name. At a sign from Dan Yack, José-Pinto fired a few rifle-shots.

Ping, poof, paff.

Dan Yack walked away, pensive, cringing at each detonation.

Pfaff! came the echo from the direction of the sea.

Dan Yack walked away, pensive. He was thinking of the men he was about to lure down there, to Port Deception.

I must make their livelihood for them. I must see to it that they make their fortunes. I've had enough of making money for myself.

He was ready to share everything he possessed.

I must draw up a new blueprint for the contract of engagement, pro rata for each man, and a guarantee of a twenty-five per cent share in the net profits of our new company, he thought.

He went down to the telegraph office and, at the usual counter, drafted yet another cable, not in code this time: PURCHASE LATEST TYPE PHONOGRAPHS IN ALL COUNTRIES SEND BLANK CYLINDERS I HAVE MY WHOLE LIFE TO RECORD.

Tak-taktak-taktak-tak-tak-tak, the Morse apparatus interpreted his words.

Dan Yack went back to the Pourquoi Pépita?, began drinking again and playing the cats' orchestra.

Then, at about midnight, instead of going to the casino, he went up to his room and started making love again.

Ushu—a-i-a—*ushu*, sobbed the exhausted Indian girl.

TUEBDEOFRA MYOJKRHAR, cabled Dan Yack.

Meanwhile, on the other side of the ocean, Gonzalo Hortalez junior was active. He followed Dan Yack's instructions to the letter, and every one of his undertakings met with success.

Already the first whale-catcher, built to the new design, was *en route* for Chiloé, as well as two large cargo ships that were carrying the materials for the construction of the whaling-station. In New York they embarked the famous machinery for flensing the whales and, on the London Stock Exchange, whaling shares were falling vertiginously.

Someone was making a clean sweep behind the scenes.

A sensational crash was imminent.

The chips were down.

Dan Yack's establishment at Port Deception was favoured by an early spring that year. They hastened the thaw by laying charges of gun-cotton in order to blow up the ice-floes that blocked the entrance to the port and by mining the fast-ice around the great interior basin.

Customarily, the whalers arrive at Port Deception towards the end of December. This year the whaling-station was ready to go into operation by 15th November, and the two hundred labourers who had built it were now levelling the terrain where Community City was to be built.

Dan Yack's whale-catchers had launched their campaign as early as 1st December, and when the Norwegians arrived in their turn, they found Port Deception already in full swing. Six German colliers were unloading mountains of coal and the three chimneys of the whaling-station were smoking.

On Christmas Eve Dan Yack officially inaugurated his city.

A small dynamo provided temporary power for the solitary lamp-post at the entrance to the whaling-station. This was a surprise Dan Yack had prepared for his men in place of the traditional Christmas tree. The bulb winked feebly in the midnight sun.

A gramophone, crouched down at the level of the water, blared out popular tunes all night long.

Then it was back to work.

The summer at Port Deception was short. Rorquals were present in great numbers, they pursued them far to the south. Nothing interrupted the feverish activity of the little colony, except, at rare intervals, a battle with the Norwegian crews. These fights most often took place on a Sunday morning, when the men went down to do the water fatigue.

At the end of February the two fleets separated, those of Dan Yack's new company, the S.B.C., going to hunt, as they had in the past, along the coasts of Chile and in Magellanic waters, and the Norwegians in the seas around the Cape of Good Hope. Only some sixty workers remained at Port Deception, together with Dan Yack and Herr Doktor Schmoll, to set up the by-products factory and turn this folly into a reality by creating an industry in the Antarctic seas and, what was more, a *new* industry! Herr Doktor Schmoll performed miracles.

He was a genius of invention and adaptation, with a lively mind ever alert for new opportunities. Ingenious and practical, he tackled every problem boldly, head-on, and always found a solution that was both elegant and childishly simple. He did not shrink from any difficulty. He was also a daring gambler and Dan Yack professed the greatest admiration for him.

Thanks to him, the by-products factory was now in operation. During this first winter it produced mostly glue and fertilizer, and samples of the finest quality linoleum. Schmoll perfected his manufacturing process and achieved a considerable economy in fuel for lighting and heating both the town and the whaling-station by exploiting the volcanic resources of the island. The numerous hot-water springs, which reached temperatures as high as eighty degrees, were channelled, and Schmoll put the thirty-one fumaroles, which emitted fierce jets of gas and steam, to an infinite variety of uses. For example, it was his brainwave to use the emissions which gave off sulphuretted hydrogen as a vulcanizer for treating the whale white, erroneously called 'spermaceti', and to make this adipocere into an artificial ivory, hard, dense, non-flammable, as malleable and transparent as heated horn, much cheaper and more sumptuous looking than celluloid and a very advantageous substitute for this material in the manufacture of binding for books, albums, missals and psalters, paper-knives, passe-partout, crucifixes, electrical insulation, watertight joints for engines, combs, pipes, necklaces, bracelets, dominoes, billiard balls, chess sets, luminous dials, windscreens, transparent panels, knife-handles, toothbrushes, hairbrushes, etc., handles for walking-sticks and umbrellas, accessories for telephones, orthopaedic equipment, etc. etc., and items for coachbuilding.

With the return of spring came the whale-catchers, who unloaded a vast amount of equipment and brought Dan Yack his first mail from

Europe. There was still no letter from Hedwiga, but, on the other hand, a consignment of gramophones, all the latest records and a big automaton from the firm of Gebrüder Fugger. Amongst other items of news, Hortalez informed him that, armed with the first concession from the British Government, he had just filed an action against the Norwegian Company, whose sole aim was to ensure that they were definitively banned from the Port Deception fishing grounds.

In the event, when the Norwegians arrived, the bulk of their fleet berthed in Admiralty Bay on George I Island or at Morrel Point on Clarence Island. Because of this, fights between seamen were much less frequent, and in fact, by the end of the season, forty-seven Norwegian sailors had deserted their own company to come and spend the winter with Dan Yack and work in his whaling-station.

During this second winter in Community City everyone was too busy to notice the long-drawn-out night. The whaling-station roared and the by-products factory was going full blast. Schmoll installed a gut-works and a workshop for making ropes and nets; he also initiated the manufacture of heavy waterproof garments cut from whale-skins. He was equally successful in extracting a beautiful dye, of buttercup yellow, from the digestive residue of the whales. Dan Yack marvelled at all these labours.

In the third year the Norwegians put in no more than a token appearance at Port Deception. Their company had been thoroughly discomfited. Hortalez had won his court case at the first hearing. He had been able to prove that the Norwegian Company had never paid the Governor of the Falkland Islands the dues that Britain levies on fishing rights in the South Shetlands, the Orkneys and part of Graham Land. Because of this serious handicap, the Norwegians had no desire to pursue the matter in court; they had already made conciliatory overtures, and discussions between the two sides had begun.

The whalers who had brought this good news in the spring departed in the autumn carrying orders, plans and proposals for a new, intensive and methodical fishing campaign, for new manoeuvres on the Stock Exchange, for the setting up of new industries as well as for the expansion and general progress of affairs already in hand. Amongst other suggestions, Dan Yack recommended that Hortalez should get the S.B.C.'s concession extended to cover all the archipelagos in this fishing zone, from Elephant Island in the north to the Biscoe Islands in the west and the coast of Föyn in the east, taking the

Antarctic polar circle as the southernmost limit of its activity; he stressed the urgency of dispatching new fleets, equipped with modern machinery, to these new grounds; their focal point, temporarily at least, would be a large factory ship stationed at Port Lockroy, which Charcot had just discovered. In this same mail-bag Dan Yack announced that Schmoll had just succeeded in producing a synthetic, industrial ambergris, and that he was now seriously tackling the question of canning whale-meat.

In the fourth year of the S.B.C.'s existence the Norwegians asked for terms and, by the fifth, their company had been totally absorbed.

In the sixth year Gonzalo Hortalez junior came to spend the summer at Port Deception.

From out at sea, nothing could be seen at first but a huge black cloud hanging over the island; then, as you approached, you could make out the three chimneys of the whaling-station, which pierced this cloud at different points like three long knitting-needles stuck into a skein of dirty wool. From close to, you could no longer see anything but the whaling-station, with its muzzle open on to the flensing plan, its entrails exposed, angry, raging, with sudden explosions of steam, loud snarls, the continuous crunching of its formidable jaws and the deafening sound of a million sea-birds taking wing. In a horseshoe around it, turning away, squat, low, empty and abandoned looking, the brand-new but already soiled town disappeared behind mounds of coal, pyramids of barrels, mountains of crates and the huge rounded backs of oil-tanks.

Community City had a population of seven hundred and eleven inhabitants, and not a woman amongst them. Since Hortalez, newly married and on his honeymoon, had brought his wife with him, the young bride met with an unlooked-for triumph: Doña Heloisa Dolores Concepción Nazarea, née Ojanguren y Hijos, recently graduated from the Convent of the Sacred Heart, Roehampton, on the Thames, near London, a fragile doll from the big city, dressed in a hobble skirt and a feathered hat from the Rue de la Paix, was acclaimed by a band of rough Lascars, labourers and delirious seamen, who jostled each other in their eagerness to greet the first woman to set foot on Antarctic soil, fête her and give her a rousing ovation.

Dan Yack, who was amongst her most enthusiastic admirers, was overcome by the arrival of this young woman. All of a sudden he felt lonely, desperately lonely. What was he doing with his life? It was all very well laughing, chattering, displaying his wit, charming her with a

casually seductive air, walking with his colleague's wife through the
penguin rookery, showing her his attempts at gardening - three
meagre beds of Kerguélen cabbages, cress, edible mosses and some
alpine plants that refused to grow - and picking her the only flower
from this little polar garden (a viscous alga, a softish, brownish fucus,
full of burrs, smelling of putrefaction and leaving nasty stains on the
tips of one's fingers), showing her all over the factory of which he
claimed to be so proud, explaining to her the practical layout, the
efficient functioning, the ingenious mechanisms, taking her into the
statistics office, perorating in front of coloured graphs on the walls,
explaining the esoteric curves of the fishing season, complex and
elegant like the trajectories of comets, the continual ups and downs of
the whaling-station's productivity, which were drawn in blue, with
their angles alternately rising and falling, like gaping jaws armed with
teeth that were more ferocious, more numerous, sharper and more
menacing than the fangs of the steam-saw that tirelessly dissected the
whales on the flensing plan, making her trace with her finger the
progressively upward march of the whole enterprise and admire the
results they had achieved, showing her, on a hachured map of the
world, the distribution of the S.B.C.'s products throughout the
various countries of the globe, making her stick little flags into a map
of old Europe to indicate the extent of the advertising campaign, the
publicity and the billsticking, the expansion of new markets, the
construction of warehouses and stores in ports and at railway
stations, encircling such-and-such a city with a red crayon and
numbering it to mark the imminent opening of a sales organization
there, which would be in direct touch with the public for the purpose
of launching future shares and preaching the universal consumption
of canned whale-meat (especially the fins, to be known as whale
fillets), which would be in non-stop production from next winter
onward, it was all very well, then, for Dan Yack to show off, juggle
with figures as if they were aphorisms, paint a dazzling future for the
company, speak passionately of his policies, his life and his own
personal ideas, but it did not prevent Doña Heloisa from interrupting
him a hundred times a day to ask, even while she was putting on her
lipstick, whether he wasn't bored on this island? . . . and, each time,
Dan Yack was at a loss for words.

    No . . . no, he wasn't bored, but . . .

    He had had a casino built. The house he lived in in Community City
contained a collection of automata that was unique in the world. Even

the walls of the entrance hall were lined with them, every imaginable kind of mechanical contrivance stood in the corridors and in all the rooms. The ground floor was a huge drawing-room painted in Ripolin enamel and always lit *a giorno*, with a gaming-table complete with roulette wheel in the middle, and a billiard-table. At one end of the room was an English-style bar and, at the other, the famous replica of the cats' orchestra from the Pourquoi Pépita? Everywhere there were gramophones, set around the room instead of armchairs, and in the entire house there was not a single place to sit down. It was here that Dan Yack came and went during the long winter nights, never entertaining anyone, living without servants, making himself cocktails at the bar, drinking alone, playing alone at roulette or billiards, winning victories against himself, emptying a bottle of champagne, devising new combinations of cards, gambling systems, throws of dice, billiard cannons. Once he was well and truly sozzled, and the cats' orchestra was in full swing, he tried to break the bank, his own bank, and he roared with laughter when he saw all his martingales come to grief, even the most original ones, and he could never make out whether he was in luck or out of luck, or whether he was cheating himself, since he was both judge and accused!

. . . No, no, he wasn't bored, but . . . there was nothing he could look forward to, nothing, nothing, nothing . . .

The sixth winter was particularly long and rigorous.

During her stay in Port Deception they had held several public fêtes in honour of Doña Heloisa, open-air balls in which everyone participated and the young woman was danced off her feet. On the eve of the day fixed for her departure sixty-nine men came to seek out Dan Yack in his office. They demanded to be paid off, so that they could embark with the Hortalezes and 'go and find wives', as they put it.

Dan Yack let them go. But, this time, instead of amusing himself as usual in his casino, he fell to indulging in day-dreams and, for the first time in his life, the hours seemed to pass slowly, unbearably slowly.

Dan Yack was in love.

He was sick to death of always making money. He had just put the finishing touches to his grand scheme for the workers to share in the company's profits. In spite of the stir this had caused, something in Community City had changed. There was no longer the same spirit, the same atmosphere, the same goodwill amongst the men, they were totally lacking in enthusiasm.

Even Dr Schmoll had asked for permission to leave!

But Dan Yack had not allowed the latter to go, he still needed him for the realization of so many projects, in order to ensure the fortunes of the men who had come to live on his island.

Dan Yack was in love.

The gigantic profits he anticipated from the sale of canned whale-meat no longer interested him, just as, formerly, he had attached no special importance to the routing of the Norwegian Company. These two events had been foreseen long ago and, each in its due time, had fallen into place as part of a plan mathematically worked out in advance, with no possibility of surprise.

In short, what did he want?

He wanted to found a kind of universal happiness by creating a new industry on his island, and to assure each man of maximum security by providing him with work, machinery, money and unlimited moral credit, that is to say, the chance to make a personal fortune while contributing, for as long as possible, to the general well-being of the community.

Dan Yack was in love.

Well then, the men who had left in search of wives were right. Why hadn't he thought of that himself? He would organize an immigration service for women, open a school, equip a playground. When it came down to it, that's all anyone was thinking about in Community City, they were impatiently awaiting the return of the men who had promised to come back in the spring with their wives. Women would be coming here. How long the winter seemed, they could see no end to it!

More and more frequently now, Dan Yack would telephone the laboratory to ask Dr Schmoll if he would be so kind as to keep him company in the casino.

They spent the time drinking.

Probably both men were thinking of Señora Hortalez.

'Be patient a little longer,' said Dan Yack to Dr Schmoll, who complained volubly about painful erections, a kind of priapism which gave him no rest and which, although it did not in the least cloud his mental lucidity, hindered him from devoting all his attention to a given subject and was the cause of a thousand distractions when he was trying to work. 'Be patient a little longer. At the moment, we are producing a hundred and fifty thousand tins of meat every day. When we have stepped it up to five hundred thousand, I shall set you free. Meanwhile I would ask you to devote yourself to two or three little matters that I still have in mind for the welfare of my men.'

Dan Yack was in love again. He hadn't yet admitted it to himself, but he, so tender, so grateful to nature, was once more in that state of plenitude and happiness that made him so lavish, open-handedly giving away his fortune, effacing himself, preferring to take on the humblest role, to be the lowliest of the lowly amongst a crowd of people whose happiness he wished to promote.

'You will stay and help me to organize a model day nursery, won't you, Doctor? Women will be coming here and, after this first batch of married ones, many others, chosen by my immigration service, will disembark here. They'll be simple women, young, healthy, energetic. It's unforgivable of me not to have thought of it before, I who have nothing but the welfare of my men at heart. But has it occurred to you, Herr Schmoll, that we shall have plenty of children at Port Deception, and I want a strong race, cheerful and optimistic, and that again will depend entirely on our organization and the services we provide! While we're on this subject, what do you think of my idea of having a rational diet for our kids, based on seal-liver oil, as soon as they are weaned? Incidentally, you could earn yourself some extra millions, and help the community to earn countless millions more, by adding a department of pharmaceutical specialities to all the products we already extract from the whale. We could set up the factory at Punta Arenas with Hortalez, since he's always complaining that we have deserted his old headquarters and the installations that belong to his former company. Wouldn't that keep you amused? And did you know that, in earlier times, whalers never suffered from cancer, and that they attributed anti-spasmodic properties to the humours of the right whale, to its 'flurry sweat' as they called it? Moreover, they cured themselves of all kinds of sores, tumours, ulcers, chancre and syphilis by cutting open the bladder of a male whale and taking a bath in this sac? Ah, if you made a close study of all this, you would make some discoveries, I can tell you! You see, we could feed our babies on seal-liver oil, like Eskimo babies, who are the most beautiful in the world, and I'd be their foster-father, because I shall be the one who brings the seals here.'

Dan Yack was jubilant.

'And we shall call our day nursery the Santa Heloisa Nursery! Didn't you notice that Señora Hortalez was pregnant? What, have you no eyes in your head, my friend? I certainly saw it!'

All through the winter Dan Yack remained in a state of

unimaginable exaltation, fever, moody delectation and impatience.

To love, to love secretly, without admitting it, without the least desire, without the faintest hope, is a kind of insidious disease, a smouldering incubation which gradually takes possession of the soul and brings about its demoralization. It begins with nausea, a blast of suffocating heat against whose numbing effects you put up some sort of floundering resistance. But soon you let yourself go, for there is nothing to be done and you find that you have become an anaesthetized victim. This anaesthetic affords you neither a therapeutic rest nor a sleep pierced by flashes of inspiration, nor even a long interregnum of the consciousness which could be compared to a sudden abyss of the personality, or a rupture, like a steep col, in the long chain of the various states of awareness; it is rather that your own weight drags you down, as if your double were clinging to you, making you heavy, so that you must sink down to the very depths of your being, into an eddy which carries you away, unresisting, and deposits you amidst the weeds and the swaying mosses of an unstable river-bed which the currents of the unconscious drain, shift and ceaselessly hollow out, whilst, at the same time, covering you with sand and shale and rolling you helplessly from side to side. You are drowning in your own depths, and for as long as this immersion lasts, all the Ophelias, all the sirens of the senses will come and nibble at your flesh. Thousands of little round mouths torment you; sponges press up against you, mould themselves to your shape, wed themselves to you; a whole world of soft little creatures, apodal, acaudate, extravagant, tickle you all over and caress you with their undulating crests, their slobbering umbellules, their transparent bellies of budding anemone-flesh, their floating stomachs, their gelatinous tentacles, their articulated eyes; you are assailed by every kind of malaise, by tics and spasms. For this sick man, suffocating underwater, each thought is a reef of black coral or a colony of polyps. His consciousness never illumines this submarine landscape - except fragmentarily - where his instinct atrophies and his sex becomes monstrous. When at last you, the patient, emerge, when you return to yourself, you are no longer the same man: you may commit suicide, be entranced by your experience, or even carry on living a humdrum life, but then it will be in a kind of ecstasy which no longer has anything in common with desire or sensual pleasure. You will be happy, but, as an individual, you will no longer know what to do with this happiness, you will be so disorientated, alien, alone in the world.

This is what happened to Dan Yack at the end of this painful winter. He was happy. He was in love. Now he admitted it to himself. But he no longer desired anything. He no longer wanted to take on any new enterprise.

Nothing is heavier, harder to bear, more difficult, more intolerable than this, and although it makes you impatient, gets on your nerves, flays you alive and keeps you, secretly, on the qui vive, nothing more closely resembles death - spiritual as well as bodily death - than this lonely sentiment of happiness. There is no possible distraction, and however much the soul may long to be greedy, try to seize hold of everything by brute force, burst out of itself, it is so full of happiness that it perpetually creates a void about itself, falls back on itself, pines away, and nothing sustains it any more except this selfsame fire, given off by itself, which is gradually consuming it and will eventually reduce it to ashes. You can no longer possess anything, nor reach out for anything without losing your balance. Happiness bores, fatigues, sates you, and the feeling of being happy soon cloys and makes a man old before his time. Like lightning, it paralyses and isolates him. In his solitude, everything seems to him alien. No longer can he mingle in the lives of his fellow-men, except out of habit, or as a chore, or out of a sense of duty, and, without in the least wishing to treat them with contempt, he hands out alms or distributes largesse among them, but without philanthropy, without love, without charity, like those lords of ancient times who, out of condescension, deigned to appear at the village fête and chat man to man with the peasantry, and throw purses of gold to them, or, like the traveller of today who allows himself to be taken on a visit to a native village, out of boredom or indifference, or simply because it is part of a prearranged tour, for he is without curiosity, expects to gain nothing from the spectacle or from the people; local colour and exoticism mean nothing to him, he is utterly sated and blasé, for, wherever he goes, it is always the same, and this distraction, far from being a relaxation, exhausts him.

God, Dan Yack had had enough of it, but he could not leave! There was no possible way out. And now it was all the same to him, yes, he didn't care one way or the other. He could not leave Port Deception; where would he go, what could he do?

Leave? For what purpose?

Dan Yack was succumbing to the powerful influence of the Antarctic, its inhuman allure, its grandeur; he cherished his solitude and, above all, those long, interminable winter nights when he threw reason to the winds, and those white nights when it was so good to be alive, living, as it were, on another planet, those interminable summer nights that were about to recommence.

As soon as the sun returned, and long before the arrival of the whale-catchers for the seventh fishing season, Dan Yack went out seal hunting every day. He embarked alone on his electric yawl, crossed the fairway before dawn and was immediately lost in the sea-mists.

The heavy swell covered him with spray.

He was alone, without a thought in his head, sitting at the tiller with his precision rifle across his knees.

Gusts of wind buffeted him. An ice-floe bumped against his boat. He pressed imperceptibly on the controls, the boat turned gently or accelerated slightly. He heard the penguins calling. In spite of the squalls of wind, the eddies of snow, a drizzle of sunshine, banks of fog which fused or tumbled down like an avalanche as he came up to them, jets of colour in the sky or at the level of the water, Dan Yack steered straight ahead, as if in a dream, his engine droning a lullaby. Nine times out of ten he returned home with an empty bag, having forgotten everything (even to light his pipe) and never having dreamed of firing a shot; from the open sea, he brought back nothing but images of breaks, rents and tears, of an immense outflowing, a perpetual beginning again, a formidable dissolution in which everything drifted away, the air, the wind, the water; of a current continually turning in circles, a crazy turbulence, a flux and reflux, an ebb and flow that made him giddy. He set foot on dry land, but he had no idea why he had come back to Community City.

There he was, like an idiot.

They brought him their reports.

The whaling-station had produced so much; so-and-so had caught his arm in the flywheel of the burnishing machine; the first whaling fleet had arrived; three married couples had disembarked; one woman was already pregnant; a profiteer had set up shop in the town; there had been a ball and a battle, some men had seized a whale-boat by force and had left for the mainland, Dr Schmoll had gone off with them. . . . Dan Yack listened to all this distractedly and, in reply, issued his orders mechanically. There was just one thing he was in a hurry to do - leave again!

He supervised the recharging of his batteries and jumped into his yawl the moment everything was made ready.

All that was required for the orderly running of the whaling-station could be obtained by applying to the office: Dan Yack had left instructions for the new fishing campaign with Jeffries; as for the injured man, he would be evacuated at the end of the season and would be awarded his disability pension in accordance with the new scale; moreover, this summer everyone would get a productivity bonus; there was no need to worry about Dr Schmoll's defection, he would be coming back; a second whale-boat would be diverted to establish liaison between the island and Ushuaia, and anyone who wanted to make a trip to the mainland need only put his name down, so that the office staff could work out a roster, and he, Dan Yack, would give one hundred pounds to any man who came back with a bride; he also undertook to stand godfather to every new-born infant; any woman who was pregnant could move into his house, into the casino; a crèche would be established, to be called the Santa Heloisa Crèche; everything had been catered for. . . . Phew! Here he was, out at sea again.

He hugged the coast, hearing the boom of the undertow.

The days were much longer now and the light was brightening day by day. He took advantage of this increased daylight to glide into Corbeta Cove or to blow up an ice-field which stretched far to the south. This was the favourite resort of an immense herd of seals. Against the snow their sleeping bodies looked like dirty stains on a sheet. Every pleat was soiled with crystallized excrement, like sugar candy. Dan Yack, having moored his boat, walked amongst the herd, provoking the beasts and choosing his victims. There were some seals who scarcely batted an eyelid as he passed; others, with decayed jaws and manes as bald as the head of an old philosopher, grunted as he approached; the females rushed to defend their pups, the adolescents gambolled in front of him, playing leapfrog and contorting their flippers; the solitaries and the tough old bachelors pivoted on the spot and watched his progress from a distance. Dan Yack discharged his rifle at point-blank range. He chose the fattest specimens, pregnant females or nice plump virgins. When he had about one hundred laid out stiffly, he slit them from top to bottom, opened their bellies and tore out their livers. He had to make several journeys to load all these viscera into his boat. He stank of hot blood and bile.

He pushed the boat out again.

Now, Dan Yack likes to linger out at sea, for, with the prolonging of the dusk, which becomes more noticeable each day, comes a rich abundance of marine life, and this makes a striking contrast to the bleakness of the barren coast, still mantled in snow and frost. Microscopic algae, Radiolaria, provide nourishment for the innumerable organisms that compose the plankton, that lactescence of the larval forms of all creatures. These organisms, the crustaceans, the coelenterates, the echinoderms are, in their turn, the prey of fish. The surface of the sea is disturbed by the passage of shoals of anchovies, pursued by carnivorous species which in their turn are pursued by seals, sea-lions and furious killer whales. The fish also nourish the colonies of fish-eating birds that whiten the cliffs and the islands – diving, Adelian and Papuan penguins, great skua, brazen giant petrels, seagulls, cormorants and terns of all species. The whales swim in pairs and, every now and again, a little schooner belonging to the S.B.C. fires its harpoon-bearing shell. Each time the cannon booms, the whaling-station answers with a blast on its siren, its distant panting, the deafening grind of its whale-capstan, its endless chain and its muffled intestinal rumblings that are like an earthquake.

Intoxication! Dan Yack lets the boat drift. He allows himself to be carried away, and not only in his imagination, as in the days when he was on board the *Green Star* and listened to the record of the sea-lion, which stung him out of his lazy mood and roused all his hunting instincts, but, this time, carried away in reality, in a physical movement in which the great seasonal rhythm of nature, mixed with a cadence of industry, sweeps him on, yawing, lurching, weaving figures of eight, circles and spirals, and it tosses him, shakes him, while Dan Yack, abandoning the controls, gesticulates, begins to sing, to yell into the wind, cry out at the top of his lungs, whistle between his fingers, shout hurray, intoxicated, but struck to the heart with loneliness.

Yes, it was all the same to him now, except, however, this teeming life at sea, this living richness, as superabundant as it was incomprehensible, which the fleets of the S.B.C. were dedicated to massacring for him, which his factories reduced to zero and which he himself, personally, tracked down to the death. It was all the same to him, yes, except this communion with death.

Death.

Dan Yack thought of it often.

'Doña Heloisa? The only thing I can do is kill her,' he said to himself.

The idea of murder flashed through him like the sun on the ice-field, like this sun that no longer set.

To kill.

To kill himself.

Everything was decomposing.

The summer was already on the decline.

It was one of those diamantine days that come only once during the season in these high latitudes. The horizon was fathomless.

The pelagic waters were of an indescribable transparency, illumined to their lower depths by patches of phosphorescence that sparkled, spun round, then suddenly bubbled up and burst with the painful, intolerable pressure of liquid air. There was nothing the eye could fix on. Everything was intensely blue and the sky infinitely deep. The sun yawned like a shell with a pearl in its hinge.

Everything was melting.

It was hot. Even sultry.

Everything was pearly, iridescent, until it darkened to a putrescent purple amidst murky vapours of plombagine veined with long striations of orange and deep red.

Everything was dissolving into a multicoloured stain, a luminous ray, a blurred target.

Dan Yack thought of death.

An iceberg drifted close by, flashing like a burning glass, concentrating all the oblique fires of space upon him. Its crests were livid, chamfered and, with the blazing crevasses and the sea-green grottoes that riddled its surfaces, it was like a great luminous crystal. Dan Yack had been watching it for some time, hypnotized, when he saw it oscillate suddenly on its base and turn turtle. The entire mass melted away amidst geysers of foam, plunging, immersing itself completely before reappearing keel uppermost, dirty, foul, ravaged by the waters of the sea, bloated, riven, full of rotting teeth and black stumps, and with all the aspect of some shameful disease, bloody, poisonous and discoloured owing to the diatoms that had tarnished its base.

What a revelation!

It struck Dan Yack at once that it was his own life he had just seen capsizing, with everything that had carried him up to the present moment, his feelings, his pride, his insouciance, his joy; it was all coming to grief, swirling round before his eyes, withered, tarnished, rotten, carried away in a magma of mud and putrescent debris.

He had lost his bearings; with regard to things, to the nocturnal aspect of nature and the human soul, he would never again find his feet, no, never more would he rediscover his equilibrium, his stability, his jubilant personality, his lucidity, his point of view; from now on he, too, would travel keel uppermost, to melt away slowly, little by little crumble to pieces, until he disappeared at a single gulp into the brackish, stinking brine.

To die, yes, to die.

To be scattered, dislocated and, like that porous iceberg, to annihilate oneself suddenly by deliquescence.

To vanish.

Mechanically, Dan Yack took hold of the tiller and headed for the port.

He accepted everything.

Yes.

Even the idea of crime.

And what else could he do, he who had no more hope?

Besides, it would soon be winter.

When Dan Yack had stored away ten thousand seal livers, he closeted himself in the lab and emerged no more.

To hell with everything!

He burst out laughing and started drinking.

He drank.

He didn't want to see anybody.

His only distraction consisted in making his preparation of seal-liver for the new-born babies. He watched over his retorts, his glass test-tubes in which the steaming blood cooled down, drop by drop, before passing through a filter and coagulating. He stirred his receptacles and cut up the residue, a concentrated reddish-brown jelly, into little cubes, which he then pressed into irons in the form of a honeycomb to reduce them to tablets and stamp them with a double impression: on one side, the initials of his company, S.B.C., and on the other, in effigy, the head of a chubby baby.

Dan Yack thought of nothing, but he was haunted by an obsession: death.

Yes, death.

So, Dan Yack drank.

What good was it, to yearn for other things, what good?

Drink.

... (This is how one suddenly falls into habits of idleness, debauchery and drunkenness in a new town, or in a country in which one has landed for the first time. The simple impression of being

disorientated, in an alien land, is sufficient to knock you off balance,
make you hesitate and push you, not into a side-street, but rather into
a well-worn thoroughfare, where you lose yourself. You walk around,
stroll up and down, looking about you. In all innocence, you find that
the twilight is the most beautiful, or the most unwholesome, in the
world. Every day you walk past such-and-such a fountain and you
invariably stop beneath the same tuft of palms, or you stand for hours
on end at the corner of a street, come rain, come shine, on account of
some woman you have only half glimpsed, or some odour on which
the life of the streets comes to rest like a swarm of flies. What is it that
comes into your mind all of a sudden, and what is this unlikely
memory that springs up, this feeling of *déjà vu*? What an impression!
What a counter-shock! The more unexpected this is, the more likely it
is to be repeated hundreds of times, and it is always repeated in an
identical form, more and more imperious and tyrannical, yet more
and more disturbing and obscure. You can do nothing but obey. You
are bound to succumb to this titillation that is carrying you on
towards a discovery, leading you at a gentle trot, donkey fashion, with
all sorts of interruptions and diversions and an incalculable number of
halts, before tipping you out, unseating you, abandoning you there,
on the spot, all alone, face to face with yourself. What else can you do?
You are so surprised, indignant, ashamed, that you reach the point
where you are no longer aware of it, and next day you find yourself
sitting in the same place, and the day after, and so on for days and days
on end. You observe yourself. You think things over. What wearisome
repetition! This idling about, which was so enchanting at the
beginning, this tippling, this novelty, is already old hat, it is a kind of
toxic infection, a state of sloth, a total abdication of the will, a
complete surrender. And what are you contemplating over your glass?
Nothing. Your head is full of murmurs. You listen to them. You have
already acquired the habit. You are in a state of total stagnation, total
disarray, total self-abandonment. You have already acquired the habit
and, habit being second nature, new habits are like geared-down
second nature; that is why everything imperceptibly sags and, without
a jolt or a bump, gives way, allowing the dream to encroach on real
life, to encroach in an insidious way. You may find this charming or
seductive, it may wake you up, or terrify you, or paralyse you. In any
case it is too late to put the brakes on. You let yourself go, dizzily, as if
you were in a lift going up and down a bottomless well. The past and
the future march past at top speed. You are sick of them both. You are

hamstrung. Everything slips away. There is not a single landmark you can refer to. Everything is hollow. Spinning. Overflowing. You are drunk. Everything is unnaturally close. Monstrous, crushing you, smiling at you, devouring you and engulfing itself in a huge shout of laughter. This warped laughter is the new regimen of the personality; rare indeed are those who can adapt to it, which is why there are so many pitiful derelicts amongst expatriates. They are the victims of nervous lesions which are generally attributed to the pernicious climate of foreign countries, or to the corruption of the big cities, the demoralizing contact with natives, the promiscuity of slums and de-luxe hotels, indolence, gratuitous sexual indulgence, sunstroke, overeating or malnutrition, organic deficiency, a physical inability to acclimatize, a moral lapse, whereas, nine times out of ten, they are due to the crafty injection of that first impression, a sting like a mosquito's, which infects you with yellow fever, a bite that poisons, stupefies, gorges the personality to the point of filling you with malaise and revulsion. It is due to *déjà vu* and to exile, to ancient memory, to depression and sorrow, to an impression which becomes an obsession and deprives you of all your faculties by setting before your worried conscience the agonizing problem of atavism. You are lost. Everything weighs you down. Was it in a previous incarnation? Where? Why? How? Who? The spirit searches. When did this happen before? You have already seen yourself in this landscape, under this tree, in front of this window; you have already heard the sonorities of this foreign language of which you understand not a word, but whose sense you can divine; the circumstances were identical, although you cannot recall a single precise detail and it only comes back to you step by step, as the same incidents are re-enacted. It has happened before that you have felt crushed and oppressed as you sat on this bench, facing this sea, this glass, all empty, empty, empty, and already you have asked yourself the same questions: Who? How? Why? You feel a feverish need to act, to shake yourself out of it, but you sit there, numb, because you have already acted, elsewhere, and at some other time. . . .)

Act, to what purpose? I have already known death, I have already dealt out death, I have already created death.

To what purpose?

'My ancestors were nothing but butchers!' Dan Yack said to himself, thinking of his father who committed suicide in Wiesbaden after a game of baccarat; 'my uncle, the shipping magnate, was nothing but a butcher; my grandfather, who hunted, was nothing but a butcher; my great-grandfather, that most enterprising of whalers, was nothing but a butcher; all, all my family, the early navigators, the explorers and the pilots, the bold fishermen, every last one of us has done nothing but kill, always, always, and my most distant ancestor was probably a murderer. Why can't I do as they did, where does this tenderness in me come from, this revulsion, this weakness?

'Oh, Doña Heloisa!'

A visionary in surgical gloves, Dan Yack attended to his tasks in the laboratory, his mind paralysed by the haunting of death and his hands mechanically occupied in making thousands of tablets of seal-liver oil with the effigy of a fat, smiling baby on them. And so the seventh winter passed, without Dan Yack being able to reach any conclusions whatsoever.

He was heart-broken with love.

He could no longer fight against it.

What good would it do?

He drank.

Drink.

Ach, to hell with everything!

EPILOGUE

Winter was drawing to a close. Out at sea, the spring thaw had already taken place. It was, I believe, the eighth or ninth year that I had been there. I was ready to abandon the whole enterprise, to hand it all over to Hortalez and make him, quite simply, a present of the S.B.C. I wanted to leave, and never to hear his name – or the name of Doña Heloisa – again. I had had enough.

One day the arrival of the whaling fleet was signalled. It was coming in much earlier than usual. The smoke from innumerable smoke-stacks, some of them huge, announced its approach. In Community City excitement ran high. The first to set foot on dry land was Dr Schmoll, who disembarked from a dinghy flying the ensign of the German navy. Nobody understood the significance of this display. On the contrary, I was very happy to see our doctor back again, for I had dreamed up an idea for a giant gramophone, with a needle as big as a coach-bolt. I was counting on Schmoll to construct this magnificent machine, which I planned to set up in the main square of Community City, like a bandstand. I wanted to present it to my men as a final surprise before I departed. I would not leave without fulfilling this vow. I also wanted to ask the doctor whether it would be possible to extract a material similar to ebonite, for the manufacture of gramophone records, from the residue of our whales. I dreamed of records as big as a ballroom floor.

Two hundred and seventy-five boats, thirty-seven of them large colliers, had dropped anchor in our port. Like Schmoll's dinghy, they had all hoisted their colours. Guns were trained on the town. And, although only a few of the men who disembarked were in uniform, every one of them was armed.

As I said, nobody realized the significance of this demonstration, and it was quite pointless for Schmoll to threaten me with a big revolver as I went to greet him. To deploy all these armed forces here was ludicrous in the extreme. Personally, I saw nothing more in the whole business than an unlooked-for opportunity to change my life.

When Schmoll announced that he was taking possession of the island and consequently, of my whaling enterprise, the flensing-station and the town, and that all my ships were being commandeered, I burst out laughing in his face. It seemed I was a ruined man. What a bit of luck!

The Germans' first task was to install a radio station on the island and to set up a battery of two guns at the entry to the fairway. They disembarked tons of equipment. The radio station and its antennae were rapidly erected. The Germans listened in constantly. It seemed they kept in continuous communication with the Falklands and jammed all the messages coming out of that station. They also broadcast false signals, with the ships' call-signs, so that they could not be located and charted. When the men emerged from the radio station they were always excited and laughing amongst themselves. I took no notice of them; for myself, I had no complaint against them. As far as I was concerned, I had to put up with a vulgar gang of pirates, superbly organized, it is true – and this surprised me rather, as did the authority that Schmoll seemed to wield over them, the discipline he imposed and the prestige he enjoyed. Schmoll appeared to be in expectation of grave events, but, as nothing ever happened, the Germans themselves began whale-catching and settling in for a long sojourn, for, in this kind of climate, one must always be prepared for an enforced overwintering. The whaling flourished as never before. It was a weird summer.

At Port Deception the catches had always been good. The rorquals were plentiful. There were enormous pods of them. Sometimes there were right whales, especially females with their little ones, who came from the seas around the Cape, where they liked to remain during gestation. In spite of this, it was not unusual to see the whaling fleets steaming far to the south. In the preceding year I had even sent a factory ship to anchor at Port Charcot, beyond Graham Land. This year the catch took place in the waters of Port Deception itself, never out of sight of the island. That was as far as anyone could go. *Primo*, because the Germans wouldn't have allowed anyone out, and, *secundo*, because the fast-ice surrounded and enclosed us very tightly.

It was a weird summer, not blue, but red, bright red. Everybody was red with blood.

After an early spell of good weather and a rapid thaw, which had permitted the inopportune arrival of Schmoll's fleet, the cold had launched a second, vigorous offensive. The pack-ice had re-formed. The bay-ice besieged us. There was barely one channel of open water, a ragged semicircle with a sinuous branch extending out towards the west. It seemed as if every whale in the Antarctic Ocean had made a rendezvous in this pocket of water. The men set to with a will.

What a massacre! The whales abounded. They were so numerous that we had no time to aim harpoons at them, we simply rammed them. The boats drove full steam ahead into them. From the blow-hole there would be a sudden spout of blood instead of a column of water. Hurrah! Hurrah! In a matter of seconds the men's arms, their hands, their faces were as red as their red woollen shirts.

It was nothing but men yelling, whistles blowing, shouted orders, improvised manoeuvres, mad dashes, the death-flurry of whales, giant cadavers stranded on the coastal pack-ice or tossed in the heavy swell as they were towed alongside. Thousands of sea-birds swooped down on our victims, disputing their rights with us even on the flensing-plan. What carnage! The men were drunk with blood, overwork, joy. They did a magnificent job. I worked with them.

I had drawn an unlucky number. I was working on board whale-catcher number 116, which had a German crew; they were novices and their clumsiness very nearly caused several accidents. In spite of that, I retain happy memories of those days. Those few months of intensive manual work, brutalizing and back-breaking, of over-exertion, fatigue and risks that I shared with my men certainly formed part of the finest epoch of my life.

Have you never felt that you wanted to walk up the ramp, get up there on the stage, or enter the circus arena, or roll up your sleeves and grab a tool when you've stopped in front of a building-site to watch others work? As for me, I like to put my hand to the job. There is so much joy in action. I can't restrain myself. It doesn't much matter what one does. I know how to drive a locomotive and I have been underwater in a diver's suit. What hard work! Your mind is empty. You have to know how to breathe inside the helmet in counterpoint to the rhythm of the pump that is supplying you with fresh air. And then you are never heavy enough. There is always the tendency to rise up. It is weird. Divers get good wages. They are silent types. They eat and drink heartily.

On board whale-catcher 116 I had become an expert in handling the lance. It takes a lot of strength, and still more skill, to strike the whale precisely in the hollow of the left axilla, where the pads of fat are not so thick, and ram the lance in with a single thrust, deep into the thoracic cage. If you hit the bone, the instrument glances off the shoulder-blade and you run the risk of falling into the water. On one occasion we were lashed to a large ice-floe. I had gone down in the longboat to drive the lance into a whale that was about to sink. It was an arduous operation. The whale was in an awkward position. A cable had been passed under its belly and they were manoeuvring it from the ship, at the capstan, trying to pivot it towards me. I was just gathering momentum to aim and drive in the lance when the boat struck against the ice-floe and the cable of the windlass broke. One end of the cable snapped back on me like a spring, wound itself round my neck and threw me up in a high trajectory. That day I narrowly escaped being strangled, drowned, decapitated and hanged. I still have a long scar behind my ear.

So, I lived the life of my men, that punch-drunk life in which you eat and sleep when you can, work yourself to death, and drink plenty of booze so as not to feel how your strength is ebbing away, you spend every last ounce of your energy, and you become so brutalized that you are no longer capable of thought. I was no longer thinking about anything. For my part, it could have gone on for a long time, I was quite happy. Dead with exhaustion, but happy. Without desire. chewing my quid of tobacco. Spitting. Grumbling. Getting back to work. Setting off on yet another whaling trip. Filling up my dixie. All the same, there is a certain satisfaction in killing the whale. The men enjoy the kill. They are proud of themselves. They've caught it! There is rivalry between the crews. The winner is whoever kills the most whales. They were breaking records. Killing.

Everybody was covered in blood.

What a weird summer that was!

A windy summer. With terrifying squalls of wind and fog so thick that the horizon was never clear. Port Deception was really at the end of the world. One felt utterly lost there.

One morning in late January a white boat came and dropped anchor amongst us. It was a queer shape, masted as a schooner. It was flying the American flag. Everything on board was made either of wood or of non-magnetic metals. The hull was of oak and Oregon pine, joined with pegs, or tree-nails, of acacia, with a few bronze bolts. The engine itself was made of bronze or copper. Its originality lay in this construction of entirely non-magnetic materials; it did not contain a single particle of steel or iron susceptible to the influence of the magnetic needle. It had sailed into our latitudes for the purpose of studying the phenomena of terrestrial magnetism. Its scientific cruise was destined to take it as far as New Zealand. The ship was the *Carnegie*.

And so it was on board the *Carnegie* that I left Port Deception, after being officially escorted on board by Schmoll, and it was on board the *Carnegie* that I learned that Europe was at war, that the world was at war, that it had been at war for more than six months.

Disembarking at Wellington in September, I immediately enlisted with the Anzacs.

In January 1916 I was on the Somme.

In Cow Wood.

They say the war turned everything upside-down; I believe that, most of all, it turned love upside-down.